RAZORBILL

Eighteen Kisses

Laura Jane Cassidy was born in 1986 in County Kildare in Ireland and has taken time out from her Drama studies at Trinity College Dublin to write full-time. She dislikes it when people use the Internet to cheat at table quizzes, but likes it when they use it to visit her popular blog, *laurajanecassidy.com*, where she talks about book-related matters, as well as playlists, fashion and lots of other stuff.

Books by Laura Jane Cassidy

ANGEL KISS
EIGHTEEN KISSES

LAURA JANE CASSIDY

Eighteen Kisses

razOr bill

PENGUIN

RAZORBILL

Published by the Penguin Group
Penguin Books Ltd, 80 Strand, London WC2R ORL, England
Penguin Group (USA) Inc., 375 Hudson Street, New York, New York 10014, USA
Penguin Group (Canada), 90 Eglinton Avenue East, Suite 700, Toronto, Ontario, Canada M4P 2Y3
(a division of Pearson Penguin Canada Inc.)
Penguin Ireland, 25 St Stephen's Green, Dublin 2, Ireland (a division of Penguin Books Ltd)
Penguin Group (Australia), 250 Camberwell Road, Camberwell, Victoria 3124, Australia
(a division of Pearson Australia Group Pty Ltd)
Penguin Books India Pvt Ltd, 11 Community Centre, Panchsheel Park, New Delhi – 110 017, India
Penguin Group (NZ), 67 Apollo Drive, Rosedale, Auckland 0632, New Zealand
(a division of Pearson New Zealand Ltd)
Penguin Books (South Africa) (Pty) Ltd, Block D, Rosebank Office Park, 181 Jan Smuts Avenue,
Parktown North, Gauteng 2193, South Africa

Penguin Books Ltd, Registered Offices: 80 Strand, London WC2R ORL, England

puffinbooks.com

First published 2012
001 – 10 9 8 7 6 5 4 3 2 1

Text copyright © Laura Jane Cassidy, 2012
All rights reserved

The moral right of the author has been asserted

Set in 10.5/15.5 pt Sabon MT by Palimpsest Book Production Limited, Falkirk, Stirlingshire
Printed in Great Britain by Clays Ltd, St Ives plc

British Library Cataloguing in Publication Data
A CIP catalogue record for this book is available from the British Library

ISBN: 978-0-141-33215-4

www.greenpenguin.co.uk

ALWAYS LEARNING   **PEARSON**

For my grandparents:
Paddy and Frances May
Mary and the late Patrick Cassidy
with love

Prologue

Last month I met eighteen people.

I admired seven of them,
I envied two,
I angered four,
I liked three,
I hated one.

And I kissed another.

Chapter 1

Part of me knew I was dreaming, and that part told me to pay attention. I'd been waiting for this. Ever since Sergeant Lawlor had given me the photographs a few weeks ago, I'd been expecting one of the women to contact me. And now it was happening.

We walked behind a red car. It was moving slowly, steadily. The windscreen wiper swung back and forth, sweeping away the pelting rain. I looked around, but I hadn't a clue where we were. I scanned for landmarks, hoping to see something that might help me to identify this place. I couldn't let any important information slip away. But I could see nothing apart from the narrow road and the thick undergrowth on either side of it.

She walked right beside me – any closer and our shoulders would've been touching. I watched her from the corner of my eye. A Polaroid camera hung from her neck, clinking against the buttons of her polka-dot dress. She wore the same outfit as in the photograph, but she looked even prettier now. She had a small face, full lips, beautiful eyes and deep red hair. She wore fishnet tights and stilettos that clip-clopped on the tarmac. I looked down at my own shoes:

torn pink Converse that soaked up the rain. My feet were horribly cold. Looking back on it, this dream was much clearer than the ones I'd had last year. Everything was sharper, much more intense.

I continued to watch her as we walked, but she didn't look at me. She just stared straight ahead, her eyes fixed on the boot of the car. Someone had tried to cover the licence plate with plastic, but it was starting to fall away. I could see the last two digits – one and eight. You don't cover your licence plate unless you have something to hide.

I looked around again, storing away every little detail. We were somewhere remote. I could hear no sound except for the hum of the engine, the clinking of the camera, the clip-clop of the heels. There were no road markings, no street lamps. If it hadn't been for the car lights, we would've been in complete darkness. We were on a back road somewhere, probably in the countryside. We followed the car for what seemed like an eternity, but it may have only been for a few seconds. That's the problem with dreams – you can't tell how much time has passed.

The car stopped abruptly and we stopped too. There was complete silence.

This was the kind of place where you could hear a pin drop, the kind of place where nobody could hear you scream. The driver's door opened. The radio was on low – a Cure song was barely audible through the speakers. A man got out of the car. He was wearing denims, a black jumper and a balaclava. I let out a frightened gasp.

I quickly covered my mouth to mute any more sound that might come out. I was shaking all over, but I tried to stay perfectly still. He looked around and glanced straight in my direction. But it soon became obvious that he had neither seen nor heard me. He was oblivious to both of us. He took a torch from his pocket and flicked it on, a blue beam illuminating the ground in front of him. He took another look around, then opened the boot and pulled out a heaving bin bag. He swung it over his shoulder and hurried across the road, struggling a little under the weight. In his haste the bag tore and an arm dropped out, pale and limp, the fingernails painted bright red. I felt panic rise inside me, but I had to stay calm. I took a deep breath. *Focus, Jacki, focus*. He moved away from the car and over a low stone wall. We followed as he trudged along, occasionally letting out a grunt or a sigh. I couldn't stop looking at the arm. We walked through unkempt grass for a long time, then the dream seemed to fast-forward – the surroundings suddenly switched, and we were standing beside a barbed-wire fence. The grass was so long that it almost reached my knees. I looked around, but the man was nowhere to be seen.

'Where'd he go?' I said. She didn't reply. She smiled and completely ignored my question, as if I'd never said it. I squinted my eyes, searching for him in the distance, but all I saw was blackness.

'Let me take your picture,' she said. This startled me; I hadn't expected her to speak. Her voice was strangely similar to mine. She looked young too; she couldn't have been much older than me. She held up the Polaroid camera and I stepped backwards, smiling awkwardly. The flash blinded me, sending little coloured dots dancing in front of my eyes. Then I heard something in the distance, a siren maybe. I suddenly felt dizzy and stumbled a little. Something was wrong. I felt the ground tremble, then the grass started to move under us like waves. I struggled to keep my balance, bracing myself for a fall. *This can't happen*, I thought. I had to focus. I looked over at her; she was still smiling. She looked so calm, as if this was completely normal. I started to panic when I stumbled again, my hand narrowly missing the barbed wire. The dream was closing in on itself. The sky plummeted, stars dropping like bombs beside our feet. A sound from the outside was threatening to wake me up. It wasn't a siren I'd heard, it was my phone alarm. The dream was ending too soon. There was more to come, I was sure of it. I knew I didn't have long left, so I took one last look around, but everything was in chaos. As it all collapsed around us, she whispered.

'Careful . . . You're standing on my grave.'

Chapter 2

I could hear my phone, but I couldn't see it. It was getting louder; if I didn't find it soon it was going to wake Hannah up. It had escaped from under my pillow and was now lost somewhere amidst all the clothes and magazines on Hannah's floor. I leaned over from the fold-out bed and searched through the clutter, eventually locating the phone and pushing the silence button as quickly as I could. I was so annoyed that it had dragged me out of the dream. But I was happy to be waking up in Dublin. I'd missed the city and my friends there ever since I'd moved to Avarna.

'Why . . . so . . . early?' groaned Hannah from underneath her duvet. She emerged a few moments later, remnants of last night's make-up under her eyes, her dark brown hair in messy waves. She's one of those people who looks impossibly pretty, even when they've just woken up.

'Sorry for waking you,' I said. 'I've to meet somebody in town. You get some sleep, I'll be back soon.'

Last night, after I'd finished my set in Whelan's, Hannah and I had come straight back here and spent the rest of the night chatting and eating chocolate with some really bad horror movie on in the background. I usually sleep at Gran's when I'm up in Dublin because I have my own room there, but I also like crashing at Hannah's and staying up insanely late. I'd only had a few hours' sleep, but I wasn't tired. Anticipation was keeping me awake. Sergeant Lawlor had asked to see me this morning. He knew I was up in Dublin this weekend to play a gig, and we'd arranged to meet in the city centre. It was a little unnerving, how he always seemed to know my whereabouts. And also that he wanted me to get started so soon. Unnerving – but exciting nonetheless.

'Who are you meeting?' asked Hannah.

'Just a guy,' I said casually.

'Oh?' She suddenly perked up.

'Not in that way,' I said, searching for my wash bag. 'I already have a boyfriend, remember?'

'You need a better one,' she said flatly, sinking back underneath the covers. I chose to let that particular comment slide. I didn't want to argue with her, especially not at 9 a.m. I put my phone safely on the bedside table, next to the worn copy of *An Actor Prepares* that Hannah carried everywhere. I watched as she shuffled about in the bed, trying to get back into a comfy position. Hannah disliked Nick, probably because she'd heard too much of the bad stuff. Hannah and I are very close, and so she is one of the first people I turn to when things go wrong. Over the past eight months she'd received ranting phone calls chronicling the disappointments, misunderstandings and the fights involving Nick. I hadn't told her enough about all the perfect days and the cute gifts and the incredible kisses. Also, because she lived in Dublin, she rarely saw us together. Once she got to know him better she'd realize that we're meant for each other.

'Who *are* you meeting then?' asked Hannah, reaching for her own phone.

'A . . . um . . . singer, from a band. I might be playing support for them.'

'Oh, yeah, which band?'

'Um . . . *Almost Famous*,' I said, reading the movie poster above her head. I didn't like lying to Hannah. Not just because I felt bad, but also because she's a really good actress and can spot a liar a mile away. Thankfully she was too busy checking her messages to notice.

'Never heard of them,' she said. 'Cool name though.'

I wasn't sure what Hannah would think if she knew who I was actually going to meet. She didn't know that I'd helped solve a murder that had happened in Avarna. Or that Sergeant Lawlor had heard about this and asked for my help on more unsolved cases. She wasn't even aware of my unusual abilities – I didn't know how to tell her that I was able to communicate with murdered women. I was pretty sure she didn't believe in ghosts, and I didn't want her to think I was weird. On the other hand, we'd been friends for so long that she probably wouldn't care. But Sergeant Lawlor had asked me not to tell anyone about Operation Trail, and I respected that. Colin, my best friend in Avarna, knew, of course, because I didn't keep anything from him. And Mum. But nobody else, not even Nick.

I had a quick shower and dried my hair, which was so much easier to manage now that I'd cut it above my shoulders and got a fringe. I'd also let Hannah bleach it even blonder last night, which I was kind of regretting now. It looked cool, but there was the possibility that Mum would throw a fit. She was four months' pregnant and tended to have extreme emotional reactions to things. At least I hadn't got a tattoo, so she hopefully wouldn't be too upset. I was delighted she was expecting a baby; I really wanted a little brother or sister. But she seemed more annoyed at me than usual these days, which was kind of hard to deal with. Des, her new partner, was freakishly patient, which made my impatience even more noticeable. When Des had first moved into our house in Avarna, the dynamic had been strange. Mum and I fought in whispers and I spent way too much time over in Nick's or Colin's house. My dad had died of a brain tumour when I was nine, and ever since then it had just been Mum and me. So I found it difficult to get used to the idea of Des living with us. But that had only lasted a couple of weeks. Eventually we started to feel like a family and Mum started to shout at me at full volume again.

'You were talking in your sleep last night,' said Hannah as I rummaged in my satchel.

'Was I?' I tried to sound casual. I didn't want to tell her I'd had a nightmare.

'Yeah; couldn't figure out what you were saying though. I'd never heard you talk in your sleep before.'

'It's probably cos we watched that movie,' I said. 'Pretty scary stuff.' I avoided looking at Hannah after yet another lie. I busied myself by putting on my floral dress, purple leather jacket and quickly applying my make-up.

'You know what's scary,' said Hannah. 'School.' I nodded as I swept on some lip gloss, relieved she'd changed the subject. 'I don't want to go tomorrow,' she added.

'Only three weeks left till the summer holidays,' I said excitedly. 'Then you can come visit me!'

'Or you can visit me,' said Hannah. She hadn't really taken to Avarna – even the beautiful scenery hadn't swayed her. She much preferred the city. 'Oh, I forgot to say, I'm in a play next week, if you wanna come see it.'

'What play?' I asked.

She hesitated, and so I immediately knew what the answer was going to be. One of the downsides of having an actress for a best friend is that you are pretty much guaranteed to see at least six productions of *A Midsummer Night's Dream* in your lifetime. *A Midsummer Night's Dream* set in New York. *A Midsummer Night's Dream* with an all-female cast. *A Midsummer Night's Dream* with robots.

'This is actually a really good version,' said Hannah, trying to sound as enthusiastic as possible.

'I'll be there,' I said with a sigh.

'You won't regret it! Well, you might . . . but I'll thank you in my Oscar speech.'

'Get some beauty sleep,' I said, throwing the covers over her head.

'See you later,' she said with a giggle.

I texted Sergeant Lawlor to ask where exactly we were going to meet.

Ming's, he texted back.

That's weird, I thought. Wasn't it a little early for Chinese fast food? But I trusted that the strange venue was for a reason. I stepped off the tram and walked down Grafton Street.

There were only a few people around that morning, mostly tourists pulling suitcases or staff going into shops. There was a busker playing old Irish songs near Bewley's, and others were tuning their instruments. I love walking through Dublin early on a Sunday morning – it was one of the things I missed most about it. It's quiet, so you kind of feel like it's your own city – your own kingdom. I thought I'd never forgive Mum for making me move all the way to Avarna last summer, but I'd actually grown to love my new home. Yet Dublin was still my sanctuary, a place I'd always come back to.

I passed my favourite store, Tower Records (which wasn't open yet, so I managed to retain my streak of never passing it without going in), and crossed the road. I could see Ming's neon sign up ahead, and for a split second I thought, *Go back. Pretend this never happened. Go home, turn off your phone, go back to normality.* I'd had eight months of normality, and it hadn't been so bad. But even though it was tempting, I knew for certain that I wasn't going to do that. It had already started; she was already here. I even had a familiar dull pain in my head – no doubt just a preview of what was to come. I knew that the torturous headaches and visions and panic attacks I'd endured last year were likely to revisit me. And last night's dream was so clear in my mind – her whisper, soft and haunting, playing on a loop in the back of my brain. *Careful. You're standing on my grave.*

When I stepped inside the diner, it suddenly became clear why Sergeant Lawlor had picked it. The place was deserted, apart from the people working behind the counter. The decor in Ming's was pretty minimal – the walls hadn't been painted in years and the plastic was peeling away from the tables. I'd never been in there during the day and it was odd seeing it so quiet. Sergeant Lawlor was sitting in a booth at the back and he nodded as I closed the door behind me. He was wearing a black suit and tie and looked very official.

'Hi,' I said as I sat down across from him, dropping my satchel to the floor.

'Hello, Jacki,' he said. 'Thanks for meeting me.'

'No problem.' I wondered if he guessed that I'd thought twice about coming. I suppose it didn't matter; I was here now.

'I ordered you a hot chocolate,' he said. 'Hope that's OK?'

'Yeah . . . sure,' I said, a little taken aback. How did he know about my current hot-chocolate addiction? Did he know everything about me? I decided it was probably just a lucky guess.

'The team and I are delighted you've agreed to come on board,' he said, shaking a packet of sugar into his paper cup. I looked at the stuff laid out in front of him on the table – a laptop, a sheet of paper and a blue folder, so full it looked like it was going to burst open.

'I'm happy to help,' I said. Although, come to think of it, I wasn't sure what he was expecting of me. 'Um, Sergeant Lawlor . . . what exactly will I be doing?' I asked.

'Call me Matt,' he said kind of awkwardly. 'Well, like I said on the phone, we'll take it one case at a time. I really want to get working on this one. Let's see what happens after that.'

I shifted in my seat. I was feeling a little unsure of myself – I hadn't done this professionally before.

13

He hadn't seemed to notice my discomfort, and continued. 'The first one I'd like you to work on is the Kayla Edwards case. You know the photographs I gave you? She's the girl with the –'

'Red hair?'

'. . . Yes.'

'I dreamed about her last night,' I explained.

He nodded, acting casual, but I could see the mix of astonishment and fear on his face – the mixture I seemed to evoke in people whenever I talked about this kind of stuff. He hid it especially well though.

'We should get started on this case straight away,' he said. 'If that's OK with you?'

'Yeah, sure. Deadly.'

Deadly? That probably wasn't the kind of word I should use when discussing a murder case. Well, technically it was a missing-person case, although I was pretty sure Kayla was dead. My dream certainly suggested that she was. I took a deep breath and tried not to feel anxious talking to Matt Lawlor. *You're helping him, remember?* He had this authoritative air about him – it made me trust him, but also made me a little nervous at the same time. It was going to feel strange calling him by his first name.

He handed me the blue folder.

'This is her file,' he said. 'If anybody asks, I never gave you this, you don't have it.'

CONFIDENTIAL was stamped across the front. I opened it up. Inside was the photograph he'd given me, lots of photocopied sheets of paper filled with handwriting, and other assorted cuttings. A Polaroid photo fell out of the pile and I picked it up. It was a picture of Kayla and another girl with short blonde hair. Kayla was blowing up a big pink balloon and the other girl was holding it and laughing. I could see something written on the back. I turned it round, and printed in black lettering was the following:

Kayla Edwards invites you to her 18th Birthday Party
This Thursday.
Location: Her House! 25 Sycamore Rd, Dublin 6.
Time: 8 p.m. till late.

'She went missing two years ago,' said Matt. 'On the night of her eighteenth birthday party. She left the house at twelve thirty a.m. and went to the shop with two of her friends. On their way back to the party her friends decided to go home, and they parted company with Kayla at the top of her road at approximately twelve fifty a.m. There's been no trace of her since.'

I vaguely remembered hearing about it on the news. She didn't live too far from our old house. I remembered thinking it was terrible, but then the media coverage died down and I'd forgotten about it just as quickly.

'Did they find anything?' I asked. 'Like her clothes, her bag?'

'No. Nothing.'

Great. I had a feeling this wasn't going to be easy.

Matt opened up the laptop and a little *ping* sounded as he switched it on. I looked at the invitation again.

A few minutes later he turned the laptop round so that it faced me. There were people on the screen – a video was playing. I soon realized I was watching footage from Kayla's party. Laughter and applause and giggles and screams blasted from the tiny speakers. I could see Kayla sitting on a stool. She pushed her red hair behind her ear and fixed a strap of her polka-dot dress. It looked like they were in a marquee; 'I Kissed a Girl' was playing in the background. Kayla laughed as a guy kissed her on the cheek, then another guy, then a kiss on the lips from a girl, then one from a guy, a kiss on the cheek from another girl. A line formed in front of her and others gathered round in a semicircle, laughing and clapping and cheering until the eighteenth birthday kiss was planted on her cheek. I felt kind of nauseous watching it. The happy smiles, the carefree chatter, the ignorance of what lay ahead was almost unbearable. A few hours after this film was taken she was probably dead. I had to force myself to keep watching.

As each second passed, I realized how much this group of friends looked like my own. Just a regular group of teen-agers, celebrating one of their friends' birthdays, with no clue as to the tragedy that was about to happen. This was all too real. In the picture she looked real, sure, but that was just a snapshot, a snippet of a person. And in the dream she was something else – unearthly and untouchable. But here she was just like me, laughing and shouting and dancing. I watched the seconds ticking down, my stomach churning as I saw her get off the chair and dance across the floor. I let out a sigh of relief when the video stopped. I stared at the final frame, her face frozen in a huge smile.

'Did I have to watch that?' I said, handing the laptop back.

'Yes,' said Matt. 'And you might want to watch it again.'

'Why?' I asked.

'Because I strongly suspect that her killer is in this video.'

I stared at him in disbelief, but I knew from the look on his face that he was completely serious.

He handed me a list with eighteen names on it. Several of the names had been crossed out.

'These are all the people that appear in the video,' he said. 'Twelve guys, six girls. Some left the party before she went missing, ten have solid alibis. But you should talk to the other eight, see what you can get.'

I was finding this difficult to process. He thought she'd been murdered by somebody she knew? Somebody she trusted?

'You really think one of her friends could be involved?' I said. I couldn't believe it.

'In this case I don't think we're dealing with an outsider,' said Matt. 'Right from the beginning I suspected we weren't being told the full story. I've talked to all eighteen of them myself, and things just don't add up. That's why I tracked you down, Jacki. I'd come across people with psychic powers before – they'd approached our team and offered to help, though most of their theories were ridiculous and we'd never seen any real results. But when I heard about the Beth Cullen case, how you'd helped solve a twenty-five-year-old murder, I knew I had to find you. Nobody ever thought that case would be solved, just like nobody thinks we'll ever solve this one.'

He rubbed his forehead, all of a sudden seeming quite tired. 'Plus, Jacki, I think an independent voice on this case is what we need. Someone otherwise unconnected. I need someone I can trust.'

He was putting a lot of faith in me; I hoped I wasn't going to let him down. He carried on in his serious tone.

'I think you should meet the remaining eight party guests.

This is the perfect time, as they are all in town. You should come up to Dublin next week if possible.'

'I have school though,' I said. There were only a few weeks more of transition year . . . less than a month left until the holidays, but there was no way Mum would allow me to miss any days.

'Don't worry,' he said. 'I'll sort something out.'

I didn't argue. The idea of getting time off school was really appealing, and something about his tone of voice made me believe that he really could arrange it.

I looked down at the list. Eighteen names. Eight suspects. I felt a rush of excitement – I was going to do this.

I drank the last of my hot chocolate and stood up to leave. 'How did you know I like hot chocolate?' I asked.

'Same way I knew you were playing a gig in Whelan's last night,' he said.

'Garda Intelligence?' I whispered.

'The Internet.'

I laughed. For the briefest moment, a smile flashed across his otherwise serious face, but then it was gone. 'I'll talk to you soon,' he said.

I stepped out into the street, where twice as many people were milling about now. My bag was heavy with the weight of the file. I folded the list and put it in there too, then made my way towards Grafton Street. I planned to go back to Hannah's, hang with her for a little while, then get the bus to Avarna. I was glad that I'd met up with Matt Lawlor. I wasn't nervous any more; there wasn't room for nerves. I had to stay focused. I had a case to solve.

Chapter 3

'How attached are you to your second kidney?' asked Colin. He was sprawled across my bed, on my laptop, as I sat on the floor finishing off a new song.

'Very attached,' I said, between strums.

Colin had come over to my house as soon as I got back from Dublin. I'd had an idea for a new song during the three-hour bus ride, and wanted to get the melody down before I forgot it. Colin was used to me randomly working on music and scribbling lyrics, so he didn't mind that I wasn't giving him my full attention. Besides, he was busy scheming. I'd told him it was pointless, but he wouldn't listen.

'It says here that you can get five thousand dollars for one on the black market.'

I rolled my eyes.

'Jacki, you're going to have to be a bit more flexible,' he said. 'Desperate times and all that.'

'Let's face it,' I sighed. 'I'm not going to New York.'

'I'm maid of honour,' said Colin, so seriously that I had to force myself not to giggle. 'It's my job to make sure all of Lydia's favourite people are there.'

'Well then, tell her to get married in Avarna!' I said, playing louder.

Lydia and I had become pretty good friends over the past year. She's a designer and owns a shop that sells clothes and accessories in the village, so we share a love of fashion. Colin had introduced us. Even though she is technically Colin's aunt, I guess they're more like friends too, hence he got the job of chief bridesmaid. Lydia had met her American piano-player fiancé, Seth, when he came into her shop last year. He was touring Ireland with his band and wanted to buy something to take home to his mum. They got talking about the Josh Ritter CD Lydia was playing on her stereo, and he'd left the shop with a turquoise suede clutch bag and Lydia's phone number. Six months later there was a wedding invitation in my mailbox. Ever since they'd met, I'd noticed a change in her – it was like she'd learned to trust again. Most people in the village thought the entire thing was very sudden and a little bit crazy, but I thought it was wonderfully romantic. Like Seth had said – when you find someone as awesome as Lydia, you don't wait around. They were getting married in New York, as Seth was from Brooklyn. I was so happy for her. Happy she'd found someone she loved so much. And also happy that she was moving to New York, a place she'd always wanted to go. I wanted to go there too, and hopefully I would some day. But not this summer.

I was disappointed that I was going to miss Lydia's big day, but there was one advantage to staying at home – I'd get to spend lots of time with Nick. He'd been practising a lot with his band lately so I hadn't seen him that much. Sometimes I went to watch them practise, like the other guys' girlfriends, but I never felt comfortable sitting on the spare amps in Chris's garage, smiling and nodding along to the music. I found it very hard to stay in a room full of guitars without playing one. The whole thing seemed a bit pointless anyway; I didn't get how the other girls could do it. I usually ended up bailing after fifteen minutes and going over to Emily's. When the summer came, I'd be able to see way more of Nick, out of the practice room.

'Sing your song for me!' said Colin as I hummed quietly. He sat up and smiled at me expectantly.

'OK,' I said. 'It's not finished though.' I'd been excited about the song at first, but now I wasn't so sure if I was happy with it.

'Doesn't matter,' said Colin. 'Sing it anyway.'

I took a breath and sang softly.

> You said I was your angel,
> A treasure in the dark.
> I thought I was your everything
> And that I'd made my mark.
>
> You took my heart and crushed it,
> This torture can't be true.
> Still, when I think of happiness –
> I only think of you.
>
> A tiny part of what we had
> In everything I see.
> It hurts to see you with her,
> With anyone but me.

I thought I was your angel,
A treasure in the dark.
I'd kill to be your everything
Can't stand to be apart.

I'm sure that it was love,
I couldn't stop the fall.
Pretty lies and empty words,
Now I'm nothing at all.

'Cheery,' said Colin.

I gave him a fake glare.

'It's fabulous, Jacki!' he laughed. 'Just like everything you sing.' A mischievous look crossed his face. 'Can I sing *you* something?' he asked.

'Go ahead,' I said curiously.

Colin launched into 'New York, New York', jumping up on the bed and using my hair straightener as a microphone.

This time I actually glared at him.

'It's NEW YORK,' said Colin. 'You HAVE to go.'

'The wedding's in five weeks,' I said. 'It's not gonna happen.'

I was thrilled for Lydia, but I kind of wished Colin would talk about something else for five seconds.

'There has to be a way,' he said. 'We'll find a way. I know it, I'd bet my life on it.'

There was no way I was going to New York. I'd love to go, of course, but I couldn't afford it. I didn't want to ask Mum for a loan because the baby was arriving in five months and she was always talking about how much babies cost. We'd already spent so much on the renovation of the cottage. It was worth it though; it looked beautiful and my room was just perfect – I loved the purple walls, the polished wooden floor and the multicoloured chandelier. Whatever money we had left over had been used to turn one of the spare rooms into a nursery, which was all set for the baby's arrival in October. It wouldn't be fair to ask Mum to pay for my flight to New York too. But ever since Lydia had sent out the invitations Colin had been trying to come up with a way to get me a ticket. Most of his ideas were either very improbable or very illegal.

'I think you're just going to have to accept it,' I said. 'I'm not going.'

'Well, that's not very optimistic now, is it?'

I knew Colin meant well, but his determination was also just a constant reminder that I wasn't going to be at the wedding.

I heard his phone beep. I looked up two seconds later to find it shoved right up to my face. 'Oh my god,' he said. 'Oh. My. God.'

'What?' I asked.

'He texted me. He TEXTED ME!' Colin started hyperventilating and I read the screen.

Hey, Colin, it's James. What's up? Was just wondering if you wanted to hang out this Friday night?

I smiled.

James worked in an art gallery in Sligo. He was seventeen,

very cute and Colin had been crazy about him for the past six months.

'This is brilliant!' I said. 'What are you going to say?'

'I don't know.' He sat down beside me on the floor.

'This is so exciting!' I said, bouncing up and down on the spot.

'I know.' Colin was smiling, but I could sense that he was a bit nervous.

'Reply!' I said, prodding him on the shoulder.

'Not yet,' he said. 'I don't want to seem too keen. I figure I should wait at least half an hour.'

'Then it might seem like you're over-thinking your reply though,' I said, resting my guitar against the bookshelves.

'Oh my god, you're right,' said Colin, his eyes widening. 'What should I say?'

'I dunno, er . . . yes?'

He suddenly looked concerned. 'What if he means hang out just as friends? What if he doesn't actually like me? What if I've made the whole thing up?'

'Colin, I had to look at art I didn't understand for an entire hour last Saturday because he wouldn't stop talking to you.'

'Yeah, you're right,' he said, taking a deep breath.

James seemed lovely. I had high hopes for him and Colin. It would be great if they went out – Colin deserved a nice boyfriend, and lately he was always complaining about the fact that he'd never had one. James has curly blond hair and is a little bit taller than Colin. I thought they would make the cutest couple.

'What should I say?' asked Colin. 'What says *I like you, but not a scary amount?*'

I considered this carefully. '*Hey, James, I'm great, how are you? Yeah, sure, that sounds fun . . . smiley face.*'

'You're a genius, Jacki King,' he said, his thumbs quickly tapping across the phone's screen.

'I try,' I said with a laugh. 'This is so exciting!'

'I can't believe I met someone as awesome as James,' he sighed. 'Isn't it funny how you can just end up in the right place at the right time?'

'Colin, you stalked him for six months. You made me visit that Matisse exhibition four times just so you could look at him!'

'Whatever. It worked, didn't it?' he said and then turned his attention to the phone.

I watched as he reread his text a couple of times before sending it. I considered telling him about Kayla Edwards and the case I was now working on, but I didn't want to wreck his fun. He'd only start to worry. I'd tell him tomorrow – I'd have to. He was my self-appointed sidekick, after all, and he'd been such a support to me last year, when even I didn't believe what was happening to me. I'd also have to tell Mum. They both knew that I'd met Detective Sergeant Lawlor when he'd first asked me to help the police, but they didn't know that I'd heard from him again – or that I had met him that morning in Dublin as well.

'I better go,' said Colin, after he'd pressed Send.

'OK,' I said, jumping up to hug him. 'Text me if he texts you.'

'I will,' he said. 'Sweet dreams.'

I grimaced. I knew I wouldn't be dreaming anything sweet for quite a while.

The next morning I found myself standing outside Miss Jennings's office. I had no idea why I was there. I assumed I must be in some kind of trouble – that's usually why people were summoned over the intercom to the principal's office. I frantically got rid of any 'customizations' I'd made to my uniform. I rolled down the sleeves of my blazer, then took the Thin Lizzy badges off my lapels and stuffed them into my pocket. My skirt was at least five centimetres shorter than the required length, but there wasn't much I could do about that now. I pulled up my knee socks, trying to minimize the amount of flesh that was showing. Miss Jennings was equal parts pleasant and terrifying. I suppose you had to be if you were in charge of 500 teenage girls. I tried to figure out what I could have done lately that would land me here. I couldn't really think of anything though. It was especially difficult to get into trouble in transition year – it was pretty laid back and we didn't have exams. Maybe it was because I'd been a few minutes late to music class this morning. Or because I wore too much eyeliner. Or because I'd signed Emily's petition protesting about the ratio of male to female authors stocked in the school library. Whatever it was, I hoped my punishment wouldn't be too severe. I was supposed to be meeting Nick after school, so I really hoped I'd be able to talk my way out of detention.

I listened closely, trying to catch what was happening on the other side of the door with whichever unfortunate person was in there before me. I couldn't really hear properly, only catching snippets of the conversation – 'self-destructive behaviour', 'I promise it won't happen again', and so on. I distracted myself from the agony of waiting by looking at the photographs on the wall, some of which I featured in. There was a picture of me on the hockey team and in the cast of *Grease*. The musical had been so much fun – the whole of transition year had been really. I couldn't believe it was nearly over; we had less than a month left.

The office door swung open and a second-year girl, whom I vaguely recognized, walked past, looking kind of trauma-tized. She gave me a sympathetic smile; a show of solidarity to a fellow comrade destined for similar torture.

'Come in, Jacki.' Miss Jennings knew the name of every single pupil in the school, which was incredibly cool, but also a bit weird.

'Take a seat,' she said. She was wearing a black trouser suit and her auburn hair was tied back in a tight ponytail. She looked surprisingly cheerful for someone about to give detention. I settled down on the chair opposite her. Her desk was arranged in neat piles – paper, pencils, Post-its and two silver frames facing her.

'First of all, I would like to say congratulations.'

'Er . . . thanks?' I said, with absolutely no idea why I was being congratulated. As far as I was aware, I hadn't entered any competitions. I'd come second in an open-mic contest in Sligo a few weeks ago, but I was pretty sure Miss Jennings hadn't heard about that. She tilted her computer screen towards her and started to read.

'*We are pleased to inform you that your student Jacki*

King has been chosen to intern at our magazine. Her application for work experience was successful and she is invited to begin a two-week internship in our Dublin offices, starting on May the fourteenth. We do apologize for the late announcement of our chosen interns. This was due to an administrative error. If Miss King is still interested in the placement, she should contact us as soon as possible.

'Yours sincerely, Tim Kavanagh, Deputy Editor, *Electric magazine.*

'Isn't that wonderful news?' said Miss Jennings. My brain was working really fast, trying to figure out what was happening before my body gave a signal that showed I didn't have a clue what was going on. Then it struck me – Sergeant Lawlor had arranged this. Wow, Matt worked fast – I was impressed. But had I really heard that right? *Electric* magazine?

'Are you not excited?' said Miss Jennings.

'Yeah . . . no, I'm . . . I'm really excited. Sorry, I'm just so shocked.'

'That's the music magazine, right?'

'Yes. *The* music magazine!' The one I read from cover to cover in Nick's mum's shop. The magazine whose first cover was a black and white portrait of Phil Lynott, the lead singer of my favourite band – Thin Lizzy. The magazine that so many people I knew would kill to be mentioned in. I'd heard they got sent twenty demos a day – mine was buried somewhere in their stack. I couldn't believe I was actually going to be spending two weeks in their office. Miss Jennings's phone started to ring.

'Well done again, Jacki,' she said. 'Best of luck with it.'

As I left the office, I felt excited, but also a bit anxious. I couldn't wait to see inside *Electric* magazine, and two weeks in Dublin would be great. But it also meant two weeks apart from Nick. I already saw him much less than I wanted to with all his band practice and our gigs at weekends getting in the way. I took my badges out of my pockets and fixed them back on to my blazer. I headed down the corridor to maths class, trying not to think about what Nick might say when I told him after school.

We lay on Nick's bed, propped up by pillows, our legs outstretched. Nick wasn't saying much at all, offering one-word answers when I tried to make conversation.

'How was practice yesterday?' I asked.

'Fine.'

I scooched down and put my head on his chest. Nothing. He usually twirled my hair or put his arm round me or tilted his head down and smiled, but not this time. I'd rushed to his house after school and had been really looking foward to seeing him, but now I was begining to wish I hadn't bothered. I wasn't even watching the TV, I was just lying there, getting angrier and angrier by the second. I stared at the Nirvana flag on his ceiling, thinking about how annoying this was. I'm a fairly tolerant person and not very many things irritate me. However, there are four things that make me particularly angry:

Mum barging into my room without knocking. She hasn't ever caught me doing anything, but it's the principle of it.

Discrimination. Of any kind. It really bugs me.

Bad Thin Lizzy covers. I once heard a terrible cover of 'The Boys are Back in Town' at a music festival and felt sick for days. Just because it's a good song doesn't mean you have to cover it. Listen to it, appreciate it, don't rip it to shreds.

Nick's sulky moods. I'm especially annoyed when he gets into one just before I have to do something important.

We'd been having a silent fight for the past hour – after I'd told him I was going to Dublin for two weeks. It's not as if I'd told him the full story though. I knew it was crazy. We'd been going out for almost eight months, yet something had stopped me from sharing everything that had happened to me over the last year – communicating with the spirit of Beth Cullen and now Kayla Edwards, and how I was going to help with a Garda operation. I knew everything about him: how he'd cried for three straight days after his gran died, how he was going to be a sound engineer even though his dad said he had to go to university, and how he'd graffitied the wall beside Clancy's pub, but then swore to Joe that it wasn't him. And yet, he didn't know one of the most important things about me . . .

I sighed. I totally trusted Nick to keep a secret. And I loved him, I really did, but he wasn't as open-minded as Colin. He was pretty sceptical actually. I used to be too, so I got that. But if I told him the truth now he'd think I was crazy. Certifiably insane. And I didn't want him to think that – there was no need for him to know just yet anyway. The Gardai had told me not to tell anyone and I'd already told two people. Two was enough, a nice even number that was relatively easy to control.

'You promised,' he said suddenly. 'You said you'd come to my gig next week.'

I sat up on the bed, rested my back against the wooden headboard and sighed.

'I really need to take this work experience,' I said. 'You know they review one unsigned act every month; if I work there, then there's a good chance they'll listen to my CD.' I regretted saying it as soon as I had. It sounded like I valued the slight possibility of getting a review more than going to his guaranteed headline show. Which wasn't true. But I couldn't tell him the truth – I would lose him. I would lose him over something I couldn't explain.

'But you promised you'd come on Thursday; it's our first headline gig and you know what a big deal it is to me.'

'Yes, I know,' I said. 'But I can't miss this opportunity, Nick. It's *Electric* magazine.'

'You didn't even tell me you'd applied.' He looked hurt, which made me feel even worse.

'I didn't think I'd get it,' I said.

The lies were stacking up now. It had become so easy.

'I'm going to miss you,' he said. He kissed me on the cheek. I tried not to smile, but I wasn't capable, my anger was steadily dwindling. I could feel a shift in the air, that moment when you know somebody isn't mad at you any more. I was relieved. I hated fighting with him.

'I'll miss you too,' I said, lying back down beside him.

'Then don't go,' he said, kissing me on the neck, right on my heart-shaped freckle. He always did it, and it always made me feel safe.

'I have to,' I said.

'Well, in that case, I better give you this today.' He turned round and opened his bedside locker and, to my surprise, took out a red box with a little bow on it. I wasn't expecting any presents. He didn't say anything, just handed it to me. I opened it up to find a red bracelet – a pretty design of woven stainless steel. I took it out of the box and noticed that it felt familiar.

'Is this made from –'

'Guitar strings,' he said, taking the words out of my mouth.

'That's so cool!' I said, examining it more closely. 'It's lovely, Nick, but what's the occasion?'

'It's for our eight-month anniversary. Seeing as you won't be here on the actual day, I thought you should have it now.'

I felt a pang of guilt. I'd forgotten about our anniversary. Nick always remembered – it was so sweet – and the bracelet was gorgeous. It made me so happy when he did things like that.

'Thanks, Nick,' I said. 'It's lovely.'

'Sorry for getting upset,' he said. 'I just had a whole evening planned, and it's a weekday so I figured you'd be in Avarna.'

'I'll be back before you know it,' I reassured him. I slipped the bracelet on to my wrist and snuggled into him.

'You should come over on Sunday,' he said. 'Before you go?'

'I can't,' I replied, without looking at him. 'I think my mum wants to leave really early.' Another lie to add to my collection. But maybe lies weren't so bad if they were what people would prefer to hear.

Chapter 4

Getting help from the local healer was another thing that Nick just wouldn't understand. But Ger Rapple had practically saved my life last year and I needed him again now.

The grass on the mountainside up to Ger's house was still wet with dew, and white butterflies danced through the air like confetti. I took my grey sweater out of my bag and put it on – it was a bit cold up the mountain for just a T-shirt. The stones on the path crunched under my trainers, and the only other sound I heard was birds singing in the distance. As I turned the corner and saw Ger's house up ahead, I thought back to last year, to the last time I'd walked up this way. I'll never forget that day, how I arrived at Ger's house in a panic, covered in bruises that I couldn't explain. I'd been scared to death because I couldn't figure out what was happening to me. He'd been the one to explain everything – that a murdered woman was trying to contact me, and that the phantom bruises were just one of the signs she'd used to get my attention. I'd been so frightened that day and he had helped me. I would be forever grateful.

Even though I'd come a long way since last year, and

was now much more in tune with my abilities, he was still the only other person I'd met who totally understood, and the only other person I knew who could also communicate with spirits. I needed his advice again.

When I arrived at the house, I saw Ger sitting in the garden. He spotted me, folded up his newspaper and smiled.

'Hi, Jacki,' he said brightly. 'Long time no see!'

'Hi, Ger,' I said, walking across the driveway. The garden looked beautiful – with wild flowers of different colours, and trees in full bloom, their leaves fluttering in the light breeze.

'Have a seat,' he said, pointing to the other patio chair. I sat down, taking in the amazing view across Avarna. The lake at the bottom of the mountain shimmered in the sunlight, the ruined castle standing majestically at its shore.

'Any news?' asked Ger.

'Lots,' I said. 'You were right. When you said last summer that a unique path had been chosen for me, you weren't exaggerating. Beth isn't the only spirit I have to help.' Ger gave me a knowing nod and I took the blue folder out of my bag. Officially I wasn't meant to show it to anybody, but I trusted Ger. During the past week I'd read its entire contents and now knew all the details of the case. But it wasn't so much the details that mattered, it was the feelings I would get, the signs that Kayla would give me to help her move on. I was going to use my ability to see beyond the facts that the Gardai already knew.

'This is the Kayla Edwards file,' I said. 'She went missing two years ago, on the night of her eighteenth birthday party. They'd like me to find out what happened to her.'

'Has she contacted you?' said Ger.

'Yes,' I said. 'I dreamed about her last weekend. But that's only the start of it – there are others too. A detective sergeant heard about what happened with Beth and he tracked me down a few weeks ago when I was gigging in Kilkenny. He wants me to help with Operation Trail, an investigation into the disappearance of a number of women over the last ten years. Kayla's is the first case I'll be working on.' When I said it out loud it sounded inconceivable, like I was talking about somebody else's life, but I knew that Ger would believe me.

'That's great!' he said. 'I could tell you were destined for something like this.' He seemed genuinely happy for me, in fact he actually seemed impressed. It was such a relief not to have to worry about what he would think, not to have to watch what I was saying.

'Do you have any advice for me?' I asked. 'Do you want to take a look at her file?' I held the folder out to him. He stared at it for a moment, but didn't take it.

'You're well able for this, Jacki,' he said, turning his head and looking down at the mountain view. 'I knew the first time I met you that you had a gift, one that was maybe even more powerful than mine.'

I doubted that. Ger was amazing. He'd been able to communicate with my dad, who'd died when I was younger. Ger had helped me when nobody else could. He'd told me something that only my dad could have known; I think it was my dad's way of showing me that everything was going to be OK, that I had to stop denying what was happening to me and acknowledge what I was capable of. I hadn't tried to talk to him like Ger did – it's dangerous to communicate with spirits who are at rest – but last month, when I was in the grounds of Kilkenny Castle, I think he gave me another sign. It helped me decide to get involved with Operation Trail. I knew it was the right decision, but I really wanted Ger's advice. I desperately wanted him to help me now, to give me even the tiniest bit of guidance on how to go forward with the case.

'Is there anything you can tell me?' I said. 'There's nobody else I can talk to about this kind of stuff.'

'Did you read the book I gave you?' he said. I'd almost forgotten about the small black book with its leather cover and gold lettering – *Mastering Psychic Protection*, I think it was called. It was hidden somewhere in my room.

'Not yet,' I said.

'You need to read that,' he said. 'Communicating with spirits is a dangerous business, even with the ones who don't mean you any harm. It can be very draining; you should know how to protect yourself.' Considering all the headaches and panic attacks and visions I'd had last year, I couldn't have agreed more.

'And as I said before,' he continued, 'you also have to protect yourself from the negative energies of people on this side, people who might not want the truth to be revealed.'

'What do you mean by . . . negative energies?'

Ger looked serious. 'Sometimes people direct harmful vibes at others, whether knowingly or not. If a person doesn't want the truth to come out, then they might send negative energies your way. It's called a psychic attack . . . You might never encounter one of these, but it's better to be prepared.

They can range from mild attacks that you may not even notice, to dangerous ones like the Difodi Curse – which is designed to kill and which can only be lifted by the person who performed it.'

I was starting to get scared. I think Ger noticed.

'These are very rare though,' he went on. 'Because if any information about the curse is revealed, like the reason for its existence, the curser will also incur torturous pain. I don't mean to frighten you, Jacki, but it's good to be aware of these things. One way to protect yourself is to imagine a white light round you, shielding every part of your body. Other means of protection are described in the book – you should read it.'

'I will,' I said. 'Every page.'

'And it might be a good idea to ask for something that belonged to Kayla, a piece of jewellery perhaps, to keep with you. It will help you to connect with her.'

'OK, cool,' I said. 'Is there anything else?'

Ger hesitated for a moment, but then looked straight at me. 'This might sound pessimistic,' he said, 'but don't trust everyone you meet through this kind of work. Remember that people will do anything to protect themselves, and to protect the ones they love. Always remember to take care of yourself first. Other than that, just use your ability. You are meant to do this, Jacki. Remember that, and you'll be OK.'

'Thanks,' I said. 'I really needed to hear that.'

'You'll do great,' he said. 'You can come up here any time; you know you're more than welcome. But I'm certain that you'll be able to do this by yourself – it's why you were chosen.'

Before last summer, before any of this had happened, I never thought that our paths might be laid out for us, that what we are meant to do with our lives is already decided, and I suppose I still wasn't entirely sure. After all, didn't we also have a choice? But Ger had known this would happen, he'd seen what was in store for me. I wanted to help these women; if I'd been chosen to do this then I wouldn't let them down. Ger and I sat in silence for a few more minutes, enjoying the magnificent view. I would have liked to stay longer.

'I'd better get going. I'm heading to Dublin in an hour.' I put the file back in my bag and stood up to leave.

'Have a safe trip,' said Ger with a smile and he stood up too.

'Thanks so much for everything,' I said, shaking his hand.

'Best of luck, Jacki,' he said. 'But you won't need it.'

'How long are you going away for? Three months, is it?' said Des when he saw the amount of stuff I'd just put into the boot of the car. 'Are you sure it's all going to fit in your gran's house?'

'Very funny,' I replied, then turned my attention to trying to pack it all in. There was a slight problem – my music equipment practically took up all of the space. I tried to squeeze in my suitcase of clothes, but finally decided I'd have to put it on the back seat instead.

'Where's your mum?' asked Des.

'I think she's in the bathroom,' I said. 'Morning sickness . . .'

'I wish I could have it instead of her,' he said, rushing into the house. I rolled my eyes. Sometimes Des and Mum were so disgustingly in love that it almost made me sick myself.

I never thought I'd have a little brother or sister, not after my dad died. I'd found it difficult to accept Des and Mum's relationship at first, but I was really happy for them now – at least when they weren't being super cringey. Des is very nice and would do anything for Mum, and come to think of it, he does a lot for me too. One night I was playing a gig in Galway, but the hostel I was staying in was absolutely rank. I'd got the slot at the last minute, and it was around New Year so there was nowhere else available, at least not anywhere that I could afford. At 2 a.m. I just couldn't stick it any more, and although I felt bad for waking him, I caved and rang Des. He drove the whole way to pick me up in the middle of the night. He'd jumped into the car the minute he got the call, and hadn't even stopped to change out of his pyjamas (which was totally mortifying, especially when we went to the McDonald's drive-thru on the way back, but I couldn't really give out to him). Even after that experience, I still go gigging practically every weekend. Sometimes I wonder if it'll be worth it, playing in all these random places, hardly ever getting paid, often singing to no more than a handful of people. But then I remember that I love singing and playing music – they're my passions – and I've always wanted to make them my career. Although I did seem to be taking an entirely different direction at the moment – I never imagined I'd be working with the police. Maybe my other, more unusual skills would take over.

'Jacki, Jacki!' I could hear Colin shouting before I saw him.

'Oh, I'm glad you're still here.' He ran up the driveway and bent over the car, trying to catch his breath.

'You OK, Colin?' I said, throwing my make-up bag in on top of my suitcase.

'You know how you're going up to Dublin, fighting crime and stuff – will you be back by Thursday?'

'No, I don't think so,' I said, pushing the suitcase further in so that I could fit my laptop beside it.

'Jacki, it's my second date with James on Thursday. You know that second dates are make or break! I need you to help me prepare. I need to come over here beforehand and you need to tell me what to wear and what to say and how to –'

'Colin,' I said. 'You don't need me. You'll be fine.' Their first date had gone really well. I'd heard every single detail multiple times. He and James had gone bowling, and then for dinner in an Italian restaurant in Sligo. James had walked him to the bus stop, and then they'd kissed. (Colin reckons it lasted about four seconds, but he can't be sure.) He thinks James had fun, but he can't be sure about that either, even though James texted him that night saying, I had lots of fun today, we should do it again next week. Immediately after he'd got that text Colin had run all the way up to my house, just like he'd done now. I don't think I've ever seen him look that happy. Except maybe the time we'd visited the Hoshino Yukinobu manga exhibition.

'Maybe I should come to Dublin with you,' he said. 'I don't like the thought of you doing this by yourself.'

'I'll be OK,' I said with a smile.

'Ring me if you need anything.'

'I will,' I said, just managing to close the car door. 'You should come up to Dublin for Hannah's play on Friday.'

'Yeah, she texted me about it,' said Colin. 'I can't wait.'

I liked that my Dublin friends had got to know my Avarna ones, and how we sometimes did things together. Hannah and Colin got on particularly well – they'd bonded over their mutual love of horror movies and their mutual dislike of boys who wore really tight skinny jeans. But then again, everybody loves Colin.

He hugged me. 'Some sidekick I am.'

'Don't say that,' I said. 'You're the best.' My phone beeped with a text. I took it out of my pocket and saw that it was from Sergeant Lawlor.

Kayla's sister Libby will be home this afternoon. I told her you'd call by. Address is in the file. M

'Ready to go?' said Mum from the doorway. She was wearing a pink dress and looked beautiful as always.

'Yep,' I said. 'I'm ready.'

I said goodbye to Colin, then turned round. In less than three hours I was going to be in Dublin – working at the magazine that I had always dreamed would discover my music, and using and learning even more about my supernatural abilities.

I couldn't wait.

Chapter 5

Kayla's road was only a short bus ride away from Gran's and I found it pretty easily. It was lined with sycamore trees, their leaves in full bloom, shading the parked cars from the afternoon sun. There were two-storey, red-brick houses on either side of the road; some had ivy growing up their walls, others had potted plants on their porches. They all had wooden sash windows, gorgeous mature gardens and cobblestoned driveways. I saw the one I was looking for, number 25, and crossed the street.

Ivy was wrapped round its red-brick pillars and the black iron gate was open. I walked slowly across the drive-way and up the steps to the front door. It was painted a pretty lilac colour, almost the same shade as my skirt. I tried not to look anxious; I really didn't know what I was letting myself in for. I took a deep breath and rang the bell.

I waited a few moments, fidgeting with the buckle on my satchel, until a girl opened the door. She wore a loose grey T-shirt, jeans and pink ballet pumps. She had long shiny brown hair and tanned skin, artificially so, but beautiful nonetheless. I guessed she was in her early twenties.

'Hey,' she said. 'You're Jacki, right? Sergeant Lawlor said you'd call by.'

'Yes,' I replied.

'Come in.' She smiled, which made me feel a lot better.

'Thank you,' I said, as I stepped inside. The interior of the house was just as impressive as the outside. The hallway ceiling was high, and sunlight flooded in through the window.

'I'm Libby,' she explained. 'Kayla's sister. Well, half-sister, to be precise.'

'Nice to meet you,' I said. Were those the right words to use? It wasn't like they were nice circumstances and it wasn't like she really had a choice in the matter.

'You too,' Libby said, not seeming to analyse it as much as me. 'Sorry about the mess,' she added as she led me into the huge kitchen. 'Dad and Anna are away on holiday, so we've kind of let the place go a bit . . . I would have tidied up, but I have an exam tomorrow and I'm frantically trying to revise.'

'It's OK,' I said. 'I'm sorry for disturbing you.'

'No problem at all. I always have exams, nothing new.'

'You mentioned Anna . . .' I said. 'Is that Kayla's mum?'

'Oh yeah, I should have explained. She's my stepmum,' said Libby.

She tidied up the chemistry books on the table into a pile and I looked around. There were lots of photos on the walls. Most were of Kayla and Libby and another girl with black hair, who I recognized from the video. The kitchen wasn't even that messy; there were a couple of empty bottles beside the fridge and a stack of dirty dishes in the sink. It looked a lot like my house when Mum and Des left me alone for a night, which unfortunately was hardly ever.

'Would you like tea or coffee?'

'Tea, please,' I said. I was relieved Libby was being so friendly. I'd wondered what her reaction would be like. It must be hard to have people interfering in your life all the time, to have to answer the same questions over and over again.

'It's good to see the Gardai are still working hard on the case,' she said. 'Still trying to find her. You're like . . . psychic, right?' She flicked on the kettle.

'Well . . . sort of. I can sense things. And I can see things that nobody else can. It's a gift I have . . . it's kind of difficult to explain.'

'Whatever it takes to find her,' said Libby, opening a cupboard and taking out two pale pink mugs. 'We had this other psychic guy offer us help last year; he said he knew where Kayla was. Turned out to be a complete wacko though.'

'Yeah, well, I didn't exactly offer to help – the Gardai contacted me,' I said, perhaps a bit too defensively.

'Oh yeah, I know. You look totally normal. Thanks so much for doing this; we really just want Kayla to come home.'

I nodded, kind of regretting my reaction now.

'So, Kayla is your stepsister?' I asked as Libby handed me my cup of tea.

'Yep, Dad married Kayla's mum, Anna, three years ago, a year before Kayla went missing. We moved in here with them because Anna didn't want to leave. Our house was so much nicer, but we got over it.'

I couldn't imagine a nicer house than this one. It was beautiful without being too flashy. Mum would love it, especially the antique dresser in the corner. She was always on the lookout for interesting stuff for our house, even though it had been finished for months.

Libby offered me the milk jug and I poured some into my cup.

'I knew Kayla before we were sisters though,' she said. 'We were in the same year in school and we used to hang around with some of the same people. She gets on really well with my big sister Hazel too – they have the same taste in music and stuff.' It was weird hearing her talk about Kayla like that, like she was still here. I seemed to be the only person who knew for sure that Kayla was dead. I had to remember that her friends and family were still clinging to the hope that she was alive. It was difficult, but I needed to believe that what I was doing would eventually give them closure. Besides, Kayla wanted to move on, she wanted peace, that's why I was here.

'Anyway,' said Libby, 'I'm rambling. Is there anything in particular you'd like to know?'

'Could you tell me about the night of her disappearance?' I asked. 'You had a party here, right?'

'Yeah, we had a small marquee out the back; there were loads of people here. It was a great night, up until . . . well . . . up until we realized she was gone. Everyone was having a good time; there was no drama.' I could tell that from watching the video. There didn't seem to be anything weird going on, at least not on the surface. It just looked like a normal eighteenth birthday party.

'When was the last time you saw her?' I asked. Libby took another sip from her tea before she spoke.

'It was around midnight. I was over at the patio door, having a cigarette, and I heard her and Amy talking about going to the shop. They got it into their heads that they wanted to toast marshmallows. They're always doing stuff like that: they think of something and then suddenly they have to have it. They're really, I don't know . . . spontaneous? They said they were going to the shop and that they'd be back in a few minutes. Andrew, Amy's boyfriend at the time, went with them. I wasn't even involved in the conversation, I just overheard it. It was about half one when I noticed that I hadn't seen them in ages. I just assumed she and Amy were off taking photos of stars or something . . . they're really into photography. But by two a.m. I started to get seriously worried. I called her mobile, but it rang out.'

'So her mobile was still turned on at that time?' According to the file, its last recorded location was in this area. It was possible that she'd dropped it in a struggle, but it had never been found.

'Yeah, she just wasn't answering it. I tried Amy's phone too, then Kayla again, but neither of them would answer. Calum said he could have sworn he saw them come back, so then I thought maybe they were around somewhere and I just hadn't seen them. I looked in every room in the house, went around calling her name, but I couldn't find her. I asked Calum where he'd seen her, but he was really drunk and wasn't making any sense.'

'Who's Calum?' I asked. I was interested because his name was on my list, along with Amy and Andrew's.

'He lives across the road; he's one of my best friends. He said he thought he saw Kayla in the house, but he wasn't sure. Somebody else said maybe she was off with Luke, this guy from her class that she was supposedly seeing, although she hadn't told me or Hazel about it.'

'Would she usually share stuff like that with you?' I asked. Luke wasn't one of the people I had to talk to, so he must have had an alibi.

'Well, probably not with me, but with Hazel, yeah. Maybe she was embarrassed or something. I mean, he's nice, but not really that hot. I rang him and there was no answer. I calmed down a bit then because I thought they were probably off . . . well, you know. But he rang me back half an hour later and said he hadn't seen her since he'd left the party. I finally got through to Amy, who told me she'd got a headache and had gone home with Andrew. She said they'd left Kayla at the top of the road. That's when everybody started to freak out and we went looking for her. We thought maybe she'd fallen on the way home and hurt herself. But there was no sign of her anywhere. Dad and Anna were staying in a hotel down the country and we didn't want to worry them, but by six a.m. there was still no sign of her and we'd called everybody she knows, so we decided to ring Dad and then we rang the Gardai.'

Libby's voice started to quiver and she looked like she was holding back tears.

'I'm sorry,' I said. 'This must be hard for you, having to relive it.'

'No, it's fine,' she said. 'It's fine.'

I felt really bad, but I wanted to get a clear picture of the night of the party.

'So Kayla walked back by herself?' I asked, as gently as possible.

'Yeah,' said Libby. 'Dad and Anna were furious at Amy; they still are. But we always used to walk home alone – nothing ever happens around here, like, you can see our door from the top of the road. It was a bit crap of Amy to leave Kayla alone on her birthday, but I don't blame her like everyone else does. Anybody can make a mistake – we all do things we regret; she shouldn't be punished forever just for one bad decision.'

I admired Libby's forgiveness – I wasn't sure I'd be so understanding.

'And anyway,' said Libby. 'It was probably Andrew's idea to leave her, not Amy's.'

I got the feeling Libby wasn't a fan of his.

'I love Kayla,' she carried on. 'I really do. But she is just way too trusting. If some random guy started talking to her, she'd probably stop and chat to him, that's just what she's like. And she's so small and slight too; if some psycho was watching her and just grabbed her, then she wouldn't stand a chance.' Libby took another sip from her tea. 'You heard about the serial killer, right?'

'No . . .' I said, feeling a shiver run down my back.

'So many women have gone missing without a trace here in the last ten years that some people think a serial killer is kidnapping them. They reckon he's keeping them for a while before . . . before murdering them. All these kidnappings have taken place in nice suburbs like this one, so we think that maybe this guy has Kayla. I mean, she didn't run away – she wouldn't just take off; she wouldn't do anything like that. And it doesn't look like she had an accident because there is literally no trace of her. We found nothing.'

She really thought it was an outsider. The thought that somebody from inside the circle might have hurt Kayla didn't seem to occur to her. I trusted Matt Lawlor's judgement and was prepared to accept that her killer may be in the video, even if the thought of it was almost too much to bear. But what if he was wrong? What if this *was* the work of a serial killer? I made a mental note to ask Matt more about it. I didn't know how he was able to do this, how he dealt with victims' families all the time, how he looked at the pain and helplessness on their faces. I admired him for it, but I didn't envy him at all. I hated to think how Libby was going to react if he was right, what she would do if she learned that the killer wasn't a stranger. But I guess it wasn't my job to worry about that; it was my job to help Kayla move on.

'Would you mind if I took a look at Kayla's room?' I said. I wanted to see if I could sense her there. Last year Beth had appeared in places that were important to her, so I thought maybe Kayla might visit her bedroom. If she was anything like me, she'd probably spent a lot of time there.

'Yeah, sure, it's this way,' said Libby.

I followed her up the stairs. Even though the house was beautiful, there was an eerie stillness in the air, like something wasn't quite right. It felt like it was suspended in time, just waiting for Kayla to come back. We walked down the corridor, then up a narrow spiral staircase. The steps creaked under my feet and I felt a little bit dizzy, so I held on to the black banister to steady myself.

'She has the attic room,' said Libby. 'Coolest room in the house.'

It was very cool. It was huge, and one wall was completely covered in Polaroid photographs. Photographs of Kayla, of her friends, scenery, bands, random things. Some of them were really quite striking. There was a picture of a white butterfly on a purple thistle, its slightly blurred wings suggesting that it had either just landed, or was about to take off.

'It's exactly as she left it,' said Libby. 'Anna told us not to touch anything. Not that I would – I hardly ever come up here.'

I followed Libby into the centre of the room. It was different to the rest of the house; its bright colours and organized chaos contrasted with the pastel shades and sparseness of the other rooms. There were similarities between it and my own bedroom – the giant piles of CDs, the posters on the walls, the dressing table covered with make-up supplies. It was unsettling to think that this kind of thing could happen to someone close to my age, someone like me. Libby started to look really uncomfortable. 'I actually . . . I don't think I can be in here now. It's too upsetting,' she said. 'You're welcome to look around, take as long as you need, but please don't touch anything. I don't mind, but Anna would probably notice and she'd freak out.'

'No, of course. I won't touch anything.' I said. 'Thanks for letting me do this.'

'I'll be downstairs,' said Libby. 'If you need anything, just shout.'

The room was really tidy, but I guess Kayla would have cleaned it before the party. There was a bookshelf in the corner, holding mostly photography and poetry books, and a few magazines, including some copies of *Electric*. On the bedside table was a Polaroid camera – just like the one from my dream – and a Holga camera too, the plastic back held on with sticky tape. On the glass-topped table there was a Canon camera, a tripod, a camera bag and a couple of extra lenses. Beside a pink Victorian-style doll's house was a stack of photo albums. Kayla must have really liked photography. There was also a laptop, its case covered with bumper stickers. I was tempted to open it, but Libby did say not to touch anything, and I didn't want to betray her trust.

I walked around the room again, taking in all the details. I didn't feel Kayla's presence there though. The room actually felt calmer than the others, and I definitely didn't sense her spirit there.

When I arrived back in the kitchen, Libby was leaning over one of her textbooks, her head resting in her hand.

'What are you studying in college?' I asked.

She jumped. 'Oh, sorry,' she said. 'I didn't hear you come back in . . . er, Medicine.'

'Oh, wow, where?' I said.

'Trinity . . .'

'Cool.'

'Did you . . . did you see anything when you were up there? Do you know what might have happened to her?' she asked.

'Well, I don't really work like that. It'll probably be a while before I have anything to report.'

'Oh yeah, of course. Sorry,' she said. 'Is there anything else I can do for you?'

'Actually, do you have something of Kayla's that I could borrow?' I said. 'A piece of jewellery, maybe? It might help me connect with her more easily.' I wanted to take Ger's advice and ask, even if she refused.

'Yeah, of course, wait there and I'll get you something. I'm sure Anna won't mind if it's going to help find her.' I was so relieved she'd said yes.

As I waited in the kitchen, I looked down at the refill pad on the table. The pages were filled with notes, and in the margins were doodles of hearts everywhere – big hearts, tiny hearts, hearts with arrows through them and hearts broken in two.

'Here you go,' said Libby, handing me a necklace with a silver star-shaped pendant. 'It was one of her favourites. She used to wear it a lot.'

'Thanks,' I said, popping it into my bag. 'I'll make sure to bring it back when I'm finished.'

'No problem. Thanks for calling over. Like I said, we really appreciate it.' Libby led me to the door and I said goodbye. I wasn't sorry to be leaving – I could sense the sadness in every corner of that house.

I walked up the road, taking a look back before I turned the corner. Libby waved from the doorway, where she stood holding her mobile and smoking a cigarette. I took the list out of my bag along with a pen, and put a tick beside her name. One down, seven to go.

Chapter 6

'Hello, love,' said Gran as I came into the kitchen. 'Have fun at Hannah's?' She gave me a warm smile.

'Yep,' I said. Since she just assumed that's where I'd been, I didn't correct her.

I was so tired, as my visit to Kayla's had been very draining, but when I sat down at the table I instantly felt better. It was good to be back here. I'd spent so much time in this terraced house over the years that it felt like a second home. I especially liked the kitchen, with its blue cabinets and collectable biscuit tins on the counter. And I loved how Gran was so nice to me, always stocking up on food I like and giving me pocket money and buying me stuff.

'I'm going to Bridge in a few minutes,' she said. 'You can come with me if you like.'

'Nah, I'll just stay here,' I said. 'Have an early night.'

That actually wasn't a lie. I hadn't dreamed about Kayla since last Sunday, but I assumed that was because I'd been sleeping in Avarna. Now that I was back in Dublin, where Kayla was from, I expected to dream about her. I expected to dream about her every night for the foreseeable future. I was going to get to sleep early because I wanted to experience the entire thing, uninterrupted. I also thought that if I went to bed early I might get some restful, dream-free sleep before it kicked in. I didn't want to look tired on my first day at the magazine.

'OK,' said Gran. 'Well, there's a pepperoni pizza for you, if you fancy it. I better get going.'

She kissed me on the cheek and I got the familiar smell of her expensive moisturiser. She used to let me put on a tiny bit when I was younger, and then I'd climb into her bed and watch the countdown on MTV while she read. When I fell asleep, my grandad would carry me into my own room and kiss me on the forehead before he left.

'I really like your hair like that,' she said as she went out of the door.

'Thanks, Gran!' I said. I liked my new hair too, mainly because it helped me look older than I was.

She left, and the silence that descended on the house made me feel kind of uneasy. My grandad died three years ago, and since then my gran had got involved in lots of things – volunteering in a local charity shop and taking up new hobbies. I think it helped her cope, helped fill the silence.

I took the star-shaped necklace from my satchel and put it on the table. I wondered if it would help me to connect with Kayla. Last summer, after I'd found Beth's bag, things had started to happen more quickly. I agreed with Ger, and sensed that it would be useful to have something of Kayla's to keep close to me.

After I'd finished my dinner I watched some TV, then headed up to bed. I like the spare room in Gran's house. It used to be Mum's, and when we both stay over she gets to have it, but when she's not there then it's all mine. It has a wooden floor and pink wallpaper. The dresser drawers are lined with scented paper and there's an old rocking chair in the corner. It reminds me of the carefree days when I used to stay over and spend all day playing with Gran.

I unpacked the last of my stuff, including my copy of *Mastering Psychic Protection* – the book that Ger had advised me to read. This time I was going to be prepared. I wasn't going to let headaches or panic attacks slow me down. I read some pages, but it was written in very old, complicated language and I was quite tired, so I decided to leave it for another day. I'd make sure to do what Ger had suggested though, and imagine a white light round me, protecting every part of my body. Lying there in bed, I couldn't quite shake the uneasy feeling I'd had since going to Kayla's house. Without really thinking, I leaned over, picked up my mobile and rang Nick's number. I just wanted to hear his voice – someone comforting and familiar.

'Hey,' he said.

'Hi! How are you?'

'Good,' he said, his voice suggesting that he wasn't.

'How was practice?' I asked, trying to sound upbeat, even though there was obviously something wrong.

'Fine.'

I sighed. The upbeat thing obviously wasn't working. 'Are you OK?'

'Yeah. Why?'

'You seem a bit annoyed.'

'I'm fine,' he said tightly. 'I just don't think we need to talk every night, you know? I'm kind of tired.'

'Oh, right, yeah . . . sorry,' I said, a little bit shocked.

'Night.'

'Night.'

He hung up and I got a sinking feeling in my stomach, that emptiness I felt when he did stuff like that. *He's just upset*, I told myself. *He's just upset because I'm missing his gig*. I looked down at the guitar bracelet on my wrist – a reminder that he obviously still loved me. I shouldn't be so sensitive. It was fine and he was right, we didn't need to talk every night. But still, I knew *I* wouldn't have said something like that. I could feel the anger rising inside me. I snatched my phone off the locker and texted him.

There's no need to be so moody.

I didn't regret sending it, I wanted him to know I was annoyed. I waited a few minutes, but there was no reply, no apology, no nothing. I slammed the phone down, got under my duvet and closed my eyes.

The dream was the exact same – the car, the covered-up number plate, the stilettos, the rain. We followed the man in the balaclava, over the low stone wall, but this time I wasn't staring at the arm because I'd noticed something in his back pocket. A Polaroid photo – the same one from the file. He had an invitation to the party.

The surroundings suddenly switched, and once again we were standing beside the barbed-wire fence.

'Where'd he go?' I asked. She didn't reply. She smiled and completely ignored the question, as if I'd never said it. I squinted my eyes, searching for him in the distance, but all I saw was blackness.

'Let me take your picture,' she said. She held up the Polaroid camera and once again the flash blinded me, sending little coloured dots dancing in front of my eyes. I looked around, searching for some landmark, anything that would help me to figure out where we were. I saw a tree to our right, its branches all twisted and bare as if it had been struck by lightning. Wild red roses were growing in the hedges either side of it. The sharp pointed edges of a barbed-wire fence glinted in the moonlight.

She held the photograph out to me. I leaned over to look at it, but to my surprise, I wasn't in it. Instead it was a picture of the man in the balaclava, his brown eyes staring straight at the camera. I gasped and stumbled backwards, narrowly missing the barbed-wire fence.

'Careful,' she said. 'You're standing on my grave.'

I woke up with a jolt, sweating and shaking, taking in gulps of air, as if I might stop breathing altogether. There was no serial killer, or if there was, he hadn't killed Kayla. Matt Lawlor was right: she'd been murdered by somebody who was at the party, somebody she knew. My heart was racing. I took deep breaths, trying to get the image of the man in the balaclava out of my mind. Eventually my heart stopped beating so fast, and I drifted into a restless sleep. The eyes from behind the balaclava haunted me until the morning.

Chapter 7

I rubbed the sleep from my eyes. I was exhausted from the night before, but I had to give the impression of being at least semi-ready and alert for my work experience. I checked the map on my phone again. I was confused – it told me I was outside *Electric* magazine, but I couldn't see the big bold sign I'd imagined such a famous magazine would have. People in suits hurried by, walking with purpose, and schoolkids wearing brightly coloured backpacks passed me by as I tried to decide which direction to go. I really didn't want to be late for my first day. I probably shouldn't have spent so much time eating breakfast, but Gran's scrambled eggs were just too delicious to miss. I ended up walking past the office building three times before finally spotting the tiny and discreet blue, record-shaped sign with *Electric* magazine written under it. This place was so cool it didn't even need to advertise itself to anyone. I took a deep breath and rushed inside, taking the elevator to the fifth floor.

The lobby I stepped out into was amazing. One wall was just glass, with a stunning view over St Stephen's Green. Framed covers of *Electric* hung on the walls, some dating back thirty years. There was a huge desk in the shape of a guitar inside the door and behind it sat a girl on the telephone. Her hair was styled in a neat braid and she wore lots of jewellery. Her bracelets clinked together as she talked. She covered the receiver with her hand. 'Work experience?' she asked.

'Yes – Jacki King,' I said quietly.

She pointed to the red leather sofa on the far side of the lobby, then resumed her phone conversation. 'He's in a meeting at the moment, would you like to be put through to his voicemail?'

There was a guy already sitting on the couch, flicking through the latest copy of *Electric*. He had black curly hair and glasses and was wearing jeans and a blue check shirt, its sleeves rolled up. I could see his green eyes as he looked up nervously from the magazine.

'Hey,' I said.

'Hey,' he said with a smile.

'I'm Jacki; are you here for work experience too?' He was about my age and looked just as apprehensive.

'Yeah,' he said. 'I'm Dillon.'

Up close he looked vaguely familiar and I wondered where I'd seen him before.

'I think I know you . . .' he said. 'You're friends with Hannah Murray, right?'

'Yeah . . .' I said, still not recalling where we'd met.

'I'm mates with her brother Mark,' he explained, and then it began to dawn on me.

'I thought I knew you all right,' I said. 'You look different though.'

'I cut my hair.'

'That's it.' I knew exactly who he was now. He used to hang out with Hannah's brother, reading comics and listening to music in their garage. Hannah was always complaining because they rarely let her in there, and when they did they'd make fun of her musical taste, just because she'd never heard of whatever obscure band they were listening to that week. I'd never actually spoken to him or even been introduced, but I remembered he looked a lot different back then – his hair was really long and used to kind of take over his face. I hoped he wasn't as pretentious as Hannah had described.

'So, you want to be a music journalist too?' he said.

I realized I should probably fake an interest in journalism. I wouldn't tell him that I really wanted to be a singer-songwriter.

'Yeah, maybe,' I said. 'I thought this would be interesting anyway.'

'But you don't actually want to work on a music magazine?' he said, sounding surprised.

'Well, I'm not sure yet, but music *is* my life.'

He looked at me like I was crazy.

'What?' I asked self-consciously.

'No offence,' he said, 'but you do know that loads of people would kill for this internship? Why did you apply if you don't really want to work here?'

'Um . . . well, isn't the whole point of transition year to try things you might not normally do?' I couldn't believe I was actually quoting Miss Jennings, but how dare he talk to me like that.

'So how'd you get this?' he asked. 'Does your dad work in the music industry or something?' he added with a grin. He probably didn't mean it in a bad way, but I couldn't help but be offended.

'No, actually, my dad's dead,' I said bluntly. 'Does yours?'

'Sorry,' he muttered and looked away awkwardly.

I heard my phone beep in my bag and took it out, hoping it would be Nick. It was Mum, wishing me luck. I texted her back, then we sat in silence. I tried not to let this Dillon guy get to me, but I couldn't help feeling annoyed. And I wished Nick would text me. I couldn't believe he still hadn't apologized. I wasn't having a good time with boys this week it seemed.

After a few minutes a blonde-haired girl came into the lobby. 'Hi,' she said. 'I'm Ellie, assistant to the editor.'

We introduced ourselves and she shook our hands. She was wearing high-waisted shorts, a white T-shirt, dusky pink brogues and a gold necklace that said ELLIE, which was good, because the second she said her name it went out of my head. I could feel Dillon looking at me, but I didn't make eye contact. I couldn't believe I'd have to spend two whole weeks with him. He *was* just as irritating as Hannah described.

'Follow me,' said Ellie. We walked behind her into a room with over a dozen desks arranged in rows.

'This is team *Electric*!' she said. 'Michael, Patricia, Cliona, Paddy . . .' Each person waved or said 'Hi' to us in turn. They were all incredibly stylish. I looked down at my own purple skinny jeans and Thin Lizzy T-shirt, and wished I'd gone for something a bit more sophisticated.

'The two of you will share this desk,' said Ellie, pointing to a table in front of us with one Mac and two chairs.

'In there is the office of our editor, Tim,' she added, pointing to a door on the far wall.

'Beside it is my office, and beside that is the meeting room.' Dillon and I both nodded. 'And over there is the archive.' She motioned to a box room where hundreds of magazines were shelved. 'We'll probably get you guys to tidy that up at some stage, although we've got lots lined up, so there may not be time. Firstly, I'll give you a quick overview of what you'll be doing for the next two weeks.'

Dillon took out a notebook and I rooted in my bag for a notebook that wasn't there. I was so disorganized. I thought we'd just be photocopying stuff and making cappuccinos – I didn't think we'd have to do actual proper work. Dillon seemed to notice my panic and tore off a page from his notebook and gave it to me. I took it from him grudgingly and grabbed a pen from the desk to start writing down what Ellie was saying.

'. . . Next Wednesday is the *Electric Unsigned* showcase in Rage Rock Bar and you two will be working on the floor. We'll need you there at four p.m. till late; it's tough going, but you'll get guest passes for your friends in return.'

Dillon's eyes went wide with excitement.

'The following Wednesday we're going on location and you'll assist on a shoot. It's a cover shoot so it'll be a great experience for you both.'

'Who are you shooting?' asked Dillon.

'Willis Middleton.'

'No way!' he said.

I couldn't believe it either. I'd always found Willis Middleton fascinating – an ageing British rock star who lives in New York, but also owns a castle in Galway. He's known for his awesome bass solos and outrageous behaviour.

'Yep, it's his first interview in three years,' she said. 'And his first contact with the press since he got out of rehab. He's known to be a bit . . . sensitive, so it's really important that it goes well. Hair and make-up starts at seven a.m.'

'Have you heard his solo album yet?' I asked Ellie.

'He sent us a few tracks,' she said. 'They're awesome.'

Dillon seemed impressed that I knew about his solo venture. Not that I cared.

He resumed scribbling away, his face intense with concentration. This all sounded like a lot of fun, but I didn't want to get too excited. I had to remember the real reason I was in Dublin. I still had to talk to another seven people and hopefully solve the mystery of Kayla's disappearance before I went back to Avarna.

'You'll be working on lots of different projects,' said Ellie. 'So you'll get a feel for all the different aspects of the magazine.'

Dillon pointed to the gigantic pile of CDs beside our desk. 'Is that . . .'

'The demo pile? Yes. Paul has been away for a few days so it's building up. That can be your first task, actually, to listen to these. Arrange them into two piles – good and bad, basically. If you need anything I'll be in my office. Oh, and lunch is at one. Good luck!'

I sat down on the swivel seat nearest to me and Dillon

sat on the other one, his leg brushing off mine as he did. Our shared workspace was a bit too cramped for my liking.

'I've always wanted one of these chairs,' he whispered, spinning round. It was obvious that he was trying to make up for earlier, but I still found him super-annoying. I gave him a forced smile.

'Isn't it kind of crazy that they leave this to us?' he said, looking at the pile of demos. 'That we get to decide people's fate?'

'Yep, choose wisely,' I said, taking a CD from the top of the pile and putting on my headphones. At least if we were listening to music then I wouldn't have to talk to him.

After two hours of bad drum beats and too-long guitar solos, however, my head was just about ready to explode. I was so relieved when Ellie opened her office door and waved at me. I took off my headphones. 'Jacki, can you help me in here?' she said.

I wondered what she wanted me to do. I didn't really mind what it was as long as I got a little break from this. Dillon was so engrossed in the CD he was listening to that he didn't even look up. I walked into Ellie's office and closed the door behind me.

'I'm so glad you're here,' she said. 'I was starting to think they'd forgotten about Kayla altogether.'

For a second I was taken aback, but then it clicked. She was Eleanor Higgins, a name from my list. I didn't recognize her from the party video, but then I had only watched it once. I should probably watch it again, like Sergeant Lawlor had told me to, even if it made me uncomfortable.

'I'm Kayla's best friend,' she said, signalling for me to

take a seat. Her desk was covered in stacks of paper and CDs and magazines. 'Well, I suppose she has three, but I think she's probably closest to me. Every time my phone rings, I hope it will be her.'

Unfortunately I knew that was one phone call Ellie was never going to get.

'Do you think she ran away?' I asked.

'No, no way. I think she was taken,' she said. 'But since she went missing, I've heard of two girls who were held captive and then escaped, years later . . . not in Ireland, I know, but still. You've probably heard about the serial killer theory, but they haven't actually found any bodies. So maybe he's keeping them somewhere? Sometimes I wish we could search every house. I didn't want to stop looking, but eventually I had to. As much as I'd like to, I know I can't look everywhere.' Ellie was so composed earlier, but now she looked like she might cry. She took a tissue from the box on her desk and I looked around the office, giving her a moment to wipe her eyes. The place was chaotic, there was stuff everywhere, but there did seem to be some sort of order to it. Huge cardboard copies of recent covers of *Electric* were propped up against the walls. Gemma Hayes was on the February cover, Nick Cave in March, and Imelda May was the face of *Electric* in April. The covers were really cool. The artists were all impeccably styled; I'd have done anything to get my hands on Imelda May's red dress.

'How long have you worked here?' I asked Ellie.

'I started when I was nineteen,' she said. 'I did a diploma in journalism, then began as an unpaid intern.'

'It's a really cool job.'

'It has its moments.' She smiled meekly. 'Kayla would be so impressed if she knew I was working here,' she added. 'She's big into photography. Whenever we go to gigs she always brings her giant camera with her.'

I suddenly remembered Kayla's outstretched arm in my dream, handing me the photograph, and a shiver ran through me. I tried to block it out. I could recall the dream's details so vividly, which was useful, but also unsettling. I'd never experienced a dream quite so frightening. Well, not since last summer.

'Ellie, was there anybody at the party who you were wary of?' I asked. 'Anyone you didn't trust?'

'No, not really. It was just our friends – you needed an invitation to get in. Not that Kayla wanted it to be exclusive or anything, but her dad would only let a certain number of people into the house at any one time. Hazel's boyfriend was manning the door, making sure nobody crashed it.'

'And nobody did?'

'No, it wasn't that big a gathering. I knew every single person there.'

'Did Kayla seem upset?' I asked. I figured if Ellie was her best friend she'd be able to tell me what kind of mood Kayla was really in.

'No, she was in great form. She was enjoying the party. Yeah, she was a bit quiet, but she's like that anyway, kind of introverted. But everybody likes her. I can't think of anybody who would want to hurt her . . .'

Ellie was obviously another person who didn't suspect any of her friends. I wondered if I would know, if I would sense during any of these interviews, that I was sitting across from a killer. Probably not. After all, I hadn't sensed who the killer was last summer; I'd only figured it out when it was almost too late. But this time I had a head start – I wasn't going to ignore Kayla like I'd ignored Beth. I was going to follow the signs she gave me and I was going to do everything I could to find out what had happened to her.

'Sergeant Lawlor told me what you can do,' said Ellie. 'I hope you can find her.'

'I hope so too,' I said. There was such expectation in her eyes, it made me uneasy.

'I better get back to those demos,' I said, wanting to get out of the office. This was particularly difficult for me. I knew Kayla was dead, but I couldn't tell Ellie. I felt so bad for her. I didn't know what I'd do if something happened to Nick or Colin or any of my friends.

'Yeah, of course,' said Ellie. 'I hope it's not too boring. Sergeant Lawlor said you needed a reason to be up here, so I put in a good word.'

'No, not at all, thanks a million,' I said. 'I love music, so this is perfect.'

I left the office and sat back down. I listened to a few more CDs, including a jazz ensemble, who were actually really good. The time went by so much more quickly when the music I was listening to wasn't terrible. Before I knew it, it was one o'clock.

'See you back here at two sharp,' said Ellie as she passed our desk. She talked to us like she had earlier, like the exchange in the office had never happened, which I suppose was necessary. Nobody else could know why I was really here.

'Hey, you wanna go somewhere for lunch?' asked Dillon brightly. He picked up his bag and put it over his shoulder.

'Listen,' I said. 'It's fine about earlier. You don't have to make it up to me; I suppose you couldn't have known that my dad is dead. But I'm entitled to be here too, you know.'

'I know,' said Dillon. 'I'm really sorry. I was just nervous about starting here, and when I'm nervous I say things that I immediately regret. Let's start over, OK? Would you like to go for lunch?' He shuffled awkwardly on the spot.

'OK then, sure,' I said, picking up my own bag. 'Where do you want to go?'

'Do you like crêpes, by any chance?' he said.

'Love them.'

'Cool, follow me so,' he said, and we made our way towards the elevator.

I took a bite out of my ham and cheese crêpe. The place was packed – the waiters were calling out order numbers as they walked past the tables, balancing plates expertly on their arms. I could feel the heat coming from the huge hot plates behind the counter, where a guy was flipping crêpes with a spatula. The sweet smells of cooking batter, melting chocolate and burning sugar filled the air. We sat at a small table in the corner. It was a bit crowded, but totally worth it because the crêpes were amazing.

'Do you come up to Dublin much since you moved away?' asked Dillon, who'd already eaten half of his chicken one.

'Yeah, a good bit,' I said. 'I've played a few gigs up here.'

'I remember seeing you upstairs in Whelan's once,' he said. 'I was there with Mark.'

'Oh yeah?'

'You played a cover of "Pale Blue Eyes" . . . I remember cos it's my favourite song.'

'That was ages ago,' I said. 'Did you want to strangle me?' I added with a laugh.

'No!' he said. 'It was a really good cover.'

That was nice of him to say, I thought. I loved playing that song – it was one of my favourites too.

'Most of the time people talk so loud you can hardly hear me, and sometimes there's only, like, six people in the audience,' I said with a sigh.

'There were only six people at U2's debut gig in London,' he said with a smile. 'So you're in good company.'

I smiled too. Maybe Dillon wasn't *that* annoying after all.

I wanted to turn the attention away from me. I love singing and love performing, but I don't really like talking about myself all that much. 'So, you want to be a music journalist?' I said. 'Who do you most want to interview –'

'Hayley Williams,' he answered before I'd even finished the sentence.

'What would you ask her?'

'To marry me,' he said, trying to keep a serious face.

I laughed. I had to admit that he was kind of funny too.

'I can't believe we get to meet Willis Middleton,' he said. 'That's class.'

'He's meant to be crazy,' I said. 'Genius on bass though. Do you play anything?'

'A bit of piano, but not very well,' he said.

'Me too. Gran made me learn, but I much prefer guitar.' She still asks me to play to her occasionally; I think it's just so she can make sure that I'm still practising.'

'You should give your demo to *Electric*,' said Dillon. 'Your stuff is probably so much better than the crap I've been listening to all afternoon.'

'I sent it in to them a while ago,' I said. 'Never heard anything though.'

'I'll try to find it,' he said. 'Move it to the top of the pile.'

My phone beeped and I took it out of my bag. It was a text from Nick.

Hey babe, hope your first day's going well x

I felt a flood of relief. I was so glad Nick had contacted me. He didn't mention my angry text from last night at all, but maybe that was a good thing. I'd thought that he might apologize for being cranky, but it was probably best to just forget about it. Every couple has fights; I didn't have to turn it into a big deal. I was just so happy that everything was OK between us again.

'Oh gosh, it's nearly five to!' I said, spotting the clock on my phone. Dillon and I had been chatting so much that I hadn't noticed the time pass.

'We better get goin',' said Dillon, gulping down the rest of his Coke.

I rushed out after him, devouring the last bit of my crêpe as I ran.

Chapter 8

After work I wandered around town for a while. I was due to meet up with Matt, but that wasn't for another hour, so I had some time to kill. He'd called me earlier, during my afternoon coffee break, and said he wanted to introduce me to some of the other members of Operation Trail, and also to Kayla's other half-sister, Hazel. We were going to meet in Rage Rock Bar, where Hazel worked, and where *Electric* were having their unsigned gig next week. I'd heard lots about the bar before, but I'd never actually been inside it because they were really strict on IDs. It was famous for its Acoustic Tuesdays – on the first Tuesday of every month a different musician would play a live acoustic set. But the cool thing was you never knew who the artist was going to be until they walked out on stage. So you could get a local singer-songwriter, a famous frontman or an international superstar. The guy who owned Rage apparently knew everybody in the music business, so people like Bruce Springsteen and Joni Mitchell had played there in the past. I was really looking forward to visiting it.

As I walked around, I decided to go to a charity shop, the one where I'd found my vintage microphone and pink typewriter. I love browsing in second-hand shops because you find really cool stuff that nobody else has. You have to do some serious rooting though, because the best things are the hardest to find. As I stepped inside, the woman at the counter smiled at me, then turned her attention to the broken porcelain owl that she was gluing back together. Its head had become detached from its body.

I sifted through the clothes, the hangers scraping against the steel rail as I pushed dated blouses and sequined tops aside. There was a musty smell in the air – the kind you just can't shake from a collection of old objects. I spotted a grey Janis Joplin T-shirt hidden under a denim shirt, and took it out to have a look. It was a little bit big for me, but at one euro it was an absolute bargain, so I decided to buy it. I also looked through the small stack of books they had, searching for any music biographies. I still had lots at home that I hadn't had a chance to finish yet, but I liked adding to my collection because they were my favourite things to read. There weren't any this time, but I found a *Definitive Guide to Manga* for two euro and bought it for Colin.

As I was leaving the shop, my phone started to ring. I thought it might be Sergeant Lawlor. I searched through all the stuff in my bag and finally found it, but it wasn't him calling me, it was Hannah.

'Hey,' I said.

'You have some nerve.'

'Um . . . what?' I had no idea what she was talking about.

'When were you going to tell me that you're in Dublin?' she said, sounding very annoyed.

'Oh, sorry, Han, I've just been crazy busy and –'

'Do you know who I had to find out from? Mark. My *brother* knows more about you than I do.'

He must have been talking to Dillon. I'd forgotten how fast news travels around here.

'I'm doing work experience,' I said. 'It was sort of a last-minute thing.'

'Yeah, I heard. You're working at *Electric*? You kept that quiet. Like . . . when did this happen?'

'I only found out the other day; I've just been really busy.' I'd been so caught up in the case I hadn't even thought to tell Hannah that I was in town.

'Are you too busy to hang out now?'

'Well, actually, I have to –'

Hannah did one of her dramatic sighs.

'Tomorrow,' I gave in. 'I'll meet you after school?'

'Fine!' she said, and then hung up. I wasn't worried – she never stayed mad for long.

I put my phone in my bag and headed for Temple Bar.

I walked through the cobbled streets, past the buskers and groups of tourists, until I arrived at Rage Rock Bar. In the window there was a faded missing-person poster of Kayla, the same picture I had in my bag. Tape was peeling away from the poster's corners. I pushed open the door and stepped into an almost empty pub. A girl stood in front of the bar. She wore black skinny jeans, a studded belt and a Clash T-shirt. She was quite a bit taller than me, and her black hair was cut into a blunt bob. She was beautiful.

'Jacki, right?' she said with a smile.

'Yeah; you must be Hazel,' I said as I closed the door behind me. The floor was covered in a kind of transparent plastic and underneath it were thousands of guitar plecs, all scattered around. On the walls there were photographs of all the musicians who had played there over the years, signed and securely nailed in place. Each table was made of two old amps pushed together, and the place mats were iconic album covers. All this was pretty cool, but my eyes were transfixed on the back wall, staring at the best thing in the entire place.

'Is that an –'

'Original Thin Lizzy stage sign?' said Hazel. 'Yep. One of only three ever made.'

'Oh, my gosh,' I said. It was so striking. The letters of the band's name were made from lots of small square mirrored tiles; a few were broken or missing, but that only added to its charm. And round the edges of the letters were little light bulbs.

'I'll turn it on,' said Hazel, and a few seconds later it was illuminated, the lights reflecting off the glass, making the whole thing sparkle in the most magnificent way.

'Wow,' I said. This sign had actually hung behind Thin Lizzy when they'd played on tour, and now I was standing right in front of it.

'You a Lizzy fan?' said Hazel, motioning to my T-shirt.

'Yeah, possibly their biggest fan,' I said. 'Are you?'

'I think they're deadly,' she said. 'But Kayla is way more into them than me.'

For a moment I'd forgotten why I was there. It didn't feel right to stare at the sign any longer, so I turned back round.

'Sergeant Lawlor called,' she said. 'He mentioned they're running a little bit late, but they'll be here soon. Can I get you something to eat? We have fries, burgers . . . I'll show you a menu.'

'Oh, no thanks,' I said.

'How about a drink?'

'Sure. I'll have a Coke, please.'

Hazel walked behind the bar and poured me a glass. She moved so gracefully, every movement so effortless. She had lots of piercings in her ears, and a few tattoos on her arms, including one that said *Kayla* on the inside of her left wrist.

'Do they hurt?' I asked. 'Tattoos, I mean. I'm thinking of getting one.'

'Sort of,' she said. 'It's like a hot needle continuously jabbing into your skin. But it's so worth it . . . What are you going to get?'

'A treble clef.'

'Cool.'

She handed me the Coke and I sat up on one of the barstools.

'I got this one to remind me never to give up,' she said, pointing to her wrist. 'To remind me never to stop looking for her.' I nodded. It broke my heart to hear her say that.

'So, you ever been here before?' she said, resting her elbows on the bar.

'Nope, but I've heard about your Acoustic Tuesdays,' I said. 'They sound deadly.'

'Yeah, they're pretty cool all right. We're always sworn to secrecy about who's playing; we can't tell a soul. Rumours circulate, of course, but we can't confirm or deny them. I'll never forget the time U2 walked out there,' she said, pointing to the raised stage in the corner. 'That was crazy. We do

Acoustic Tuesdays once a month, then we have karaoke every Friday, which is usually good fun, although it does get head-wrecking after a while, listening to people crucify your favourite songs. And on weekends we get a DJ in; he plays rock and indie, mainly the popular stuff, but it's a lot better than most of the crap they play in the clubs around here.'

'How long have you worked here?' I asked.

'Since I left school,' said Hazel. 'I planned to take a year out and then go to college, but I guess I sort of fell in love with this place. Every night there's something different going on. I'm assistant manager now, so it's pretty sweet. Matt was saying you might want to ask me some questions?' she said. 'About the party?'

'Yeah, if that's OK?' I said. It was weird hearing her refer to him as Matt, like they were friends or something. I guess he would have spent a lot of time talking to her while he was working on the case though.

'Sure,' she said with a smile. She sat up on the bar and swung her legs round, so that she was sitting right beside me. 'Ask me anything.'

Hazel had such an air of confidence about her; she gave off that vibe that some people just have, like they don't really care what anybody thinks.

'The night Kayla went missing, did you notice anything strange about her?' I asked. 'Was she in a good mood?'

'Yeah, the thing is, she was in a great mood. And if she hadn't been I'd definitely have noticed, or she would have told me.'

'So you two are close?'

'Yeah, really close. We get on great, but we also have screaming matches when she steals my clothes and breaks my CD cases. We're just like regular sisters.'

'When did you first notice she was missing?'

'Well, I went to sleep kinda early. I'd been working all day and was wrecked. My boyfriend Barry and I went out to get chips around one, then we went to bed. But Libby woke me at about four a.m., saying she couldn't find Kayla anywhere. The last time I'd seen her, she was dancing with her friend Amy. I'm a bit older than Kayla and Libby, so I'd spent some of the party in my room with Barry watching TV. I didn't want to cramp their style. I was basically there to make sure the house didn't get trashed. Not that Kayla's friends are likely to do that; they're all pretty well behaved.'

'Can you remember what happened when Libby woke you?'

'Yeah, she was in a panic, saying she'd looked everywhere, but she couldn't find Kayla. I knew something was wrong straight away – you know when you just get a feeling? I called Kev, her ex, and asked if she was with him. He just said "I wish" and then hung up. Libby and I phoned all of her friends, but nobody had seen her. I remember having the horrible thought that maybe someone had abducted her. The others were out looking to see if she'd tripped and hurt herself on her way home, but I knew something was seriously wrong.' Although Hazel talked about Kayla like she was still here, I got the feeling that she wasn't as optimistic as Libby and Ellie – that she was a bit more realistic. The tattoo, especially, seemed like a remembrance of her life rather than a reminder to keep looking for her.

'Some creep did this,' she said. 'He tore our lives apart. I'm so glad you're going to find him, Jacki.'

She touched my arm. I felt so sorry for her.

There was a knock on the door. Hazel walked over to it, again moving so gracefully it was almost hypnotizing.

'Delivery for Hazel Byrne,' said the guy outside.

'Thanks, hun,' said Hazel as she signed for it. I was sure I saw the delivery guy blush. She seemed like the kind of girl who could have anyone she wanted. The kind of girl people wrote songs about. She walked back across the bar like she owned it. She was a punk-rock princess and this was her palace.

Hazel dropped the box down on the counter.

'You know,' she said, 'sometimes I wake up in the morning, and for one second I forget all this has happened. It's just so unbelievable. I thought we lived in the safest part of Dublin.'

'Libby gave me one of Kayla's necklaces,' I said, taking it out of my pocket. 'Hope that's OK?'

'Oh yeah, that's cool. She likes that one; she wears it a lot. So . . . what exactly do you do? Do you, like, use something that belongs to the person to help lead you to them?'

'Yeah,' I said. 'Something like that.'

'That's crazy. Ooh, you should meet my friend Lauren. Actually, she was at the party so you're probably going to meet her anyway. She does fortune-telling in George's Street Arcade; she's into all that supernatural stuff. Anything like that freaks me out. But I think there's probably some truth to it all.'

'Well, I know there is,' I said.

'In a way I suppose I find it comforting,' she continued. 'Even though it scares me. My mum died when I was thirteen, so I like to think there's something there after you die. I like to think that I'll see her again.'

'My dad died when I was nine,' I said. She nodded. We didn't need to say anything. No 'I'm so sorry to hear that.' We both got it; we understood.

'Did Kayla ever come here?' I asked.

'Yeah,' said Hazel. 'She loves taking pictures at the gigs, and if there was somebody playing on Tuesdays that I knew she really wanted to see I'd text her and tell her to come down. We aren't meant to tell anybody, but I know Kayla can keep a secret. One time, Robert Smith from the Cure was here, and she was so excited. She loves them. When we first moved in with Kayla and her mum, Anna, and I heard they were her favourite band, I knew we were going to get along.'

I remembered the Cure song from my dream – 'Pictures of You' – barely recognizable on the radio. It took all my concentration not to dwell on the image of the man in the balaclava.

The door of the bar opened and Sergeant Lawlor came in.

'Hi, Matt,' said Hazel cheerfully. 'Can I get you anything?'

'No, thank you, Hazel,' he said abruptly. 'I'm going to take Jacki to meet the rest of the team.' He turned to me. 'Sorry I'm late. We better get going; they're waiting for us.'

'See you soon,' said Hazel with a smile.

I followed Sergeant Lawlor through Temple Bar, across the road and over to Ming's. Again it was deserted, apart from two men sitting at a table in the corner. One looked older than Sergeant Lawlor and had a grey moustache. The other was a lot younger; he had short blond hair and was fairly good-looking, if you were into the conventionally attractive type.

I walked behind Sergeant Lawlor over to the table and sat down. 'This is Sergeant Ray Harte,' he said, pointing to the younger man. 'And this is Detective Sergeant Tony Lonergan.' They both shook my hand.

'We're happy to have you on board,' said Tony, although he didn't sound like he meant a word of it. He seemed to be eyeing me with suspicion, like I was some sort of imposter. Ray, on the other hand, smiled at me, and was considerably less intimidating.

'It's amazing what you can do,' said Ray. 'Really amazing. Delighted to have you working with us, Jacki.'

'Jacki is going to interview the eight suspects,' said Matt.

'So that's what we're calling them now,' said Tony with a smirk.

'I think Matt might be on to something with that,' said Ray. 'As you know, I've worked on the case from the beginning, and I think there's something seriously strange about the whole thing.'

'As do I,' said Matt. 'Jacki has already met with some of them, haven't you?'

'Well, just three so far,' I said. 'Her friend Ellie, and her sister Libby. And Hazel, of course. I asked Libby for an object of Kayla's; I'm hoping it will help me connect with her.'

'And she gave it to you?' said Matt.

'Yeah, she gave me a necklace. Why?'

'I'm just impressed, that's all,' he said. 'I didn't think she'd be so cooperative.'

I was glad I'd impressed him, although getting a necklace was a long way from solving a murder.

'I still think we're looking at a serial killer,' said Tony.

'You weren't there at the initial investigation,' said Matt. 'There was a lot of conferring going on. Some of the anguish hinted more at guilt than grief. It's been two years now, and they've had time to get used to the lies, practise what they're going to say. This is messy, which is why I think Jacki's help is invaluable to us right now.'

It sounded like he was trying to convince Tony that my presence was justified.

'You can't seriously think that the serial killer is a myth?' said Tony.

'Oh no, I don't. I know he's out there,' said Matt. 'I just don't think he killed Kayla Edwards.'

'I certainly wouldn't trust that Calum guy,' said Ray. 'I don't like him at all. And Andrew Hogan is a right creep.'

'What do you mean?' I asked.

'He has a record,' said Ray. 'Aggravated assault.'

'I'd prefer not to influence Jacki,' said Matt. 'Let's see what she comes up with herself.' It looked like Matt hadn't told me everything, but I suppose that didn't matter. Like he said, too much information might cloud my judgement. I was wary of jumping to conclusions, and also of ruling anybody out, for that matter.

'I better get going,' said Tony. 'Nice to meet you, Jacki,' he added, but his tone was still harsh. He put on his jacket and left.

'Sorry about that,' said Matt. 'He's a bit sceptical.' That still wasn't an excuse to be rude, but I didn't care. I knew better than to let people like him upset me. Matt believed in me; that was enough. And I was sure that when I came up with answers for Tony he wouldn't be so dismissive.

'Can I ask you something?' said Ray.

'Yeah, go ahead,' I said.

'Aren't you . . . afraid of the ghosts?' His voice turned to a whisper.

'I've learned it's the people you need to be more scared of,' I said flatly.

'Well,' said Matt, 'there's no arguing with that.'

Chapter 9

The next day Hannah and I and my two other best friends from Dublin, Sophie and Ross, sat on the grass in a circle in St Stephen's Green, enjoying the evening sunshine.

Hannah, Ross and I had been friends since primary school. And then in first year we'd tacked a poster to the noticeboard saying BAND MEMBERS WANTED. I sang and played guitar, Ross played lead and Hannah played saxophone, but we needed a drummer and a bassist. Ross had insisted on putting the poster up on the very first day of secondary school. 'What's the rush?' I'd said.

'Jacki, we can't let any Travis Barkers or Cliff Burtons slip through our fingers.' Funnily enough, ours was the only band notice up there. We'd held auditions in the auditorium at lunch.

After a half-hour of us sitting there, staring at the door, a short girl with a purple streak in her hair walked in. She was wearing black patent Doc Martens with her grey uniform, the sleeves of her jumper were rolled up and she was carrying two battered drumsticks.

'Hey, I'm Sophie,' she said. 'I hear you need a drummer?'

'Yeah, but you'll need to audition,' said Ross, eyeing her

suspiciously. She then played an awesome drum solo, and we offered her the position on the spot. It turned out she'd done a 'Drum Skills for Beginners' class when she was seven, then taught herself the rest. We'd all been friends ever since.

Electric had been fairly uneventful that day – Dillon and I had been split up and given different tasks. I'd stuffed lots of envelopes with invitations for the *Electric Unsigned* gig, and Dillon had helped with the album reviews. The sun had shone all day and the office, with its huge windows, was unbearably warm. I was happy to be outside now. While we chatted, Sophie laid back with the sun on her face, Hannah made a daisy chain and Ross checked out any girl who walked by in shorts. Luckily his and Hannah's brief romance last year hadn't affected their friendship – they sort of acted like it had never happened, which Sophie and I were happy to go along with.

The Green was packed. Some people sat by themselves, reading or relaxing; others sat in twos or lay side by side, their fingers intertwined, and the rest sat in groups like ours – pockets of people dotted across the grass. Kids ran past carrying ice pops, and tourists examined maps, trying to decide on their next stop. The super-prepared had packed sandwiches and picnic blankets; Ross let us sit on his jacket as the grass was still damp from yesterday's rain. It was perfect, but I wished Nick could have been there. I really missed him and wanted to see him, especially now that everything was all right between us.

'All I'm saying,' said Ross, 'is that you'd probably be the first to go.' Sophie had made the mistake, on this fine evening, of posing the question, 'Which one of us do you think would be most likely to survive a zombie apocalypse?'

'I would *not* be the first to go,' said Hannah, abandoning her daisy chain and dropping it on to her lap. 'And why the hell does everyone think Ross would be the last one standing?'

'He can run pretty fast,' I said, batting away a wasp that was buzzing dangerously close to Ross's head.

'And he has the whole height thing going on,' added Sophie. Ross is six feet tall, although at one point in primary school I actually towered above him. I like to remind him of that sometimes.

'Right, who do you think would be the second last to die?' asked Hannah.

'Sophie,' said Ross and I in unison.

'She's got the whole brain thing going on,' I said. Sophie was always getting top marks in school. I was good at maths and pretty good at music too, but Sophie was good at everything.

'Then Jacki,' said Ross, 'because you know there's something tough beneath that cute exterior. Sorry, Hannah, but you just don't have the street smarts.' I didn't mind them thinking I'd be third; the idea of wandering round the world with hardly anybody to share it with didn't appeal to me much anyway.

'I would too survive a zombie apocalypse!' whined Hannah. Ross looked back at her blankly.

'Say I'd survive a zombie apocalypse!' she said sulkily. 'SAY IT!'

'I'm not gonna lie . . .'

'Say iii-t,' she said, adding in some fake crying for effect.

'Fine,' said Ross, in the most unconvincing tone ever. 'You'd survive a zombie apocalypse.'

'Why, thank you,' said Hannah. 'I'd have to agree.'

I could see him in the distance, walking alone in our direction. I sat up straighter and pushed my shades on top of my head. The others hadn't seen him yet, but he'd spotted me, and he was smiling.

'I've taken a stage-combat class, you know,' said Hannah.

'Yeah, that zombie won't know what to do when you fake drop-kick him,' said Ross with a snort.

'I'm just sayin',' said Hannah.

'Please, Hannah,' said Ross. 'Don't fake karate-chop me, pleeeease.' He and Sophie burst into giggles. They were still giggling when Dillon arrived at our side.

'Hey,' I said.

'Oh, hey, Dillon,' said Hannah, throwing Ross one final glare.

'Hey, guys,' he said, taking off his glasses and cleaning them with his white T-shirt, exposing his bare stomach for a second. I looked away quickly, realizing I'd been staring. I don't think anyone had noticed.

'What you up to?' said Hannah.

'I was just picking some stuff up for my mum. I'm heading home now.'

'Wanna hang out for a while?' said Ross.

'Nah, I can't, I told Mum I'd clean the car. I better go.' I plucked at the grass, trying not to think about the fact that I would actually have quite liked him to stay. Honestly, I don't know what was wrong with me. I must have been missing Nick too much.

'See ya tomorrow, Jacki,' Dillon said.

'Yep.' I looked up to see him smiling. 'Tomorrow.'

I watched him walk away, across the grass and down the path, until he was out of sight.

'Did you hear he kissed Maggie at her party the other night?' said Sophie.

'God, that girl thinks she's it,' said Hannah.

I knew Maggie, but not very well. She was pretty, but unbearably loud.

'I heard they're going out now,' said Ross, grabbing Hannah's daisy chain and wearing it on his head like a crown.

I frowned. I didn't think Maggie was the kind of girl he'd go for, but he was single and perfectly entitled to kiss anybody he wanted to.

'I heard he called it off,' said Sophie.

'Really?' said Hannah, snatching the daisy chain back. 'Who cares?'

'So, what classes are you taking this term?' I asked Sophie, eager to change the subject. Her dad is head of the extra-mural programme at a university, and Sophie has been sitting in on night classes since she was four.

'Astronomy, divination and criminal psychology,' she said.

'Sophie,' said Ross, 'you do know that one of these days your brain is going to get so big that it will actually explode?'

'Yes, because that's clearly how knowledge works,' said Hannah.

'Don't worry, Han,' said Ross. 'Absolutely no danger of explosion with you.'

Hannah gave him the finger. I laughed. It was good to be back.

'We're studying psychopaths at the minute,' said Sophie. 'Learning their traits and stuff.'

'Cool,' I said. 'What are they?'

'They show very little or no remorse, they have a fluctuating self-image, they often engage in self-mutilation, they experience fear of abandonment . . . that sort of thing.'

'Sounds fascinating,' I said. 'Dark, but fascinating.'

'Oh, and they have such confidence in their work, and such belief that they can't do anything wrong, that it sometimes makes them reckless. It's, like, their downfall.'

'Are those night classes not just like school though?' said Ross. 'Except you don't actually *have* to be there?'

'Not really,' said Sophie. 'I love them. People just learning for the sake of it, with no end goal but to gain knowledge . . . it's beautiful.'

'No, that's beautiful,' said Ross, staring at a group of girls in sundresses strolling past.

'We learned about tarot cards in divination last week,' said Sophie. 'That was just as interesting. I know you don't believe in that sort of stuff, Jacki, but –'

Sophie was preparing herself for a rant, which I probably would have launched into a year ago.

'I dunno,' I said. 'Maybe I do.'

'You've certainly changed your tune,' said Ross.

I shrugged. I couldn't really tell them that the reason I'd become open to the idea of the paranormal was because it was literally part of my life now.

'Well, as they say, the purpose of education is to replace an empty mind with an open one!' said Sophie with a smile.

I missed hanging out like this. It was amazing how easy it was to slot back in, like I'd never left.

'Jacki,' said Ross suddenly. 'What's up with your arm?'

'What do you mean?' I said. I looked down and saw a huge scratch, running right round in a circle from one side of my elbow to the other. It looked new, like I'd cut it on something. I took off my sunglasses and inspected it more closely. I couldn't think when it had happened – I didn't remember seeing it earlier.

'Whoa, that looks nasty!' said Hannah. It really did. It definitely looked like the kind of injury you would feel happening. But then I suddenly thought of last summer, when I'd woken up one morning with my body covered in bruises. Ger had told me that it was nothing to be frightened of, that it was simply another way that Beth was communicating with me – giving me a sign. This cut was equally inexplicable. I thought maybe this was a sign from Kayla. I wasn't sure what she meant by it though.

'Oh, that's nothing,' I said, trying to brush it off before too many other questions were asked. 'Just a scratch – it happened a few days ago.' I ran my finger along the broken skin.

'It looks painful,' said Sophie, sounding concerned.

'Yeah, is it sore?' asked Hannah.

'Not really,' I said. 'It's OK.'

'Jeez,' said Ross. 'Maybe you would survive a zombie apocalypse after all.'

Chapter 10

My plans for tonight couldn't have been more different from the relaxed sunny evening I'd spent with the others. I was due to meet up with the last two people to see Kayla alive – Amy Whelan and Andrew Hogan. We were going to walk the route they'd taken to and from the shop on the night of the party, and so possibly retrace Kayla's last moments. Even though the thought of wandering around late at night with two potential suspects made me incredibly uneasy, I wanted to walk the route after dark in order to get a feel for what happened on the night of the party. Sergeant Lawlor had set up the meeting, so he knew where I was going to be, but I had to make sure Gran didn't find out.

I stood at her bedroom door, waiting for the sounds of sleep. She doesn't snore, but if you listen closely you can hear her breathing, soft and rhythmic. I moved a little closer, and sure enough there it was. I was confident that she wouldn't hear me tiptoe away. There are a few ways to sneak out of Gran's. Number one is down the stairs, out the back door and around the side of the house. It's never wise to use the front door because she's much more likely to hear that when it closes – her bedroom is at the front. And she is also one of those people who sleeps with the window open. However, you have to keep in mind that walking around the side of the house always sets off the sensor light, which has the potential to wake her. The second option is to go out of my bedroom window and step on to the flat roof of the extension. You then lean over and grab the oak tree and shimmy down it. The only problem with this is that it almost always causes the neighbour's dog to bark. They have a Chihuahua called Charles who is scarier than any dog three times his size. There was a time when Hannah refused to come over here when he wasn't tied up. I don't think he'd actually ever hurt anybody, he's just very loud. And I suppose he's not the *only* problem with this option – it's also really dangerous. I felt bad about having to sneak out of Gran's, but it was unavoidable. Although she wasn't strict on many things she was firmly against 'gallivanting' on school nights. And since she considered work experience to be in the same category as school, there was no way I could tell her I was going out.

I grabbed my bag from where I'd placed it outside my own bedroom door, and moved very quietly down the stairs. I'd decided to go out the back door. It was much less risky.

The bus was empty, apart from a couple making out down the back and a drunk guy singing up the front. I sat in the middle, watching out for my stop. The route looked different in the darkness. I noticed things that I hadn't seen the other day. Like the neon pharmacy sign, the crowded fast-food restaurants and the derelict cinema with its boarded-up windows. I felt a bit uneasy so I listened to some Thin Lizzy on my iPod to try and distract myself. A few students got on at the next stop, talking so loudly that I could hear them over my music.

'I can't believe these are still out in the shops,' said one guy, who was munching on an Easter egg.

'That's gross,' said another. 'Don't eat all of that, Marcus. I don't want you to be sick on my couch later.'

'Relax!' he said as they trampled up the stairs.

I laughed to myself; they sounded like my friends back in Avarna.

I pressed the buzzer for my stop, then took out my earphones and wound them round my iPod. I had to be fully alert. I stepped off the bus and walked quickly through the darkness.

The pizza place was small – it mainly did take-out orders – but there were a few tables. Amy was already there when I arrived. I recognized her immediately from the picture on Kayla's invitation. Her blonde hair was longer now and naturally frizzy. She was sitting up on one of the chairs at the window. She wore a purple beret and a mint-green blazer and had a book in her hand. Her slice of ham and mushroom pizza was untouched on the paper plate.

'Hi,' I said, as I sat beside her. She looked up from her book.

'Oh, hey, Jacki?' she said.

'Yes.'

'You want some pizza?'

'Yeah, I'll go get a slice,' I said.

I bought a double pepperoni and sat beside her again, glancing at the book as I rested my plate on the counter.

'Emily Dickinson,' she said, showing me the cover. 'Reading it helps me to calm down.'

'I'm sorry I'm asking you to do this,' I said. 'But knowing the route Kayla took home would really help give me a clearer picture of the whole situation.' I had to start detaching myself more from the suspects, I thought. I was getting too involved, feeling bad for asking questions, for even being there. I had a duty to Kayla, and I had to stop apologizing for it. It just wasn't easy.

'Oh no, it's not that,' said Amy. 'It's just . . . well, Andrew and I had kind of a messy break-up. We don't really talk any more.'

'Oh,' I said. 'OK.'

'Well, we talk,' Amy carried on, her words tumbling over each other. 'But just so it's not awkward for everyone else in the group. It's never one-on-one.'

I hadn't even thought of the possibility that they would've broken up. I'd just assumed that they were still going out. I wondered if it'd had anything to do with Kayla's disappearance.

'So you only kind of get along?' I said.

'I tolerate him,' she said with a sigh.

I'd only had one other serious boyfriend apart from Nick – a guy called Cian, and I certainly didn't get along with him. In fact I'd only heard from him once since we broke up. He called me to ask if I still had his Iron Maiden CD. I was pretty sure I didn't have it, but I hadn't looked very hard. I'd gone out with other people for a few weeks at a time, and I still got along really well with them. But I'd adored Cian and I suppose the more you loved a person, the more awkward it is.

Amy tensed up as soon as Andrew arrived. He wore a black T-shirt and denims and was quite tall and muscular, the kind of person you wouldn't want to be up against in a fight.

'Hey, Jacki, I'm Andrew,' he said. 'Hi, Amy,' he added, without looking at her.

'I thought we'd walk the route you guys took on the night of the party together?' I said. 'But first I'd just like to ask you some questions.'

Amy didn't react. 'Sure,' said Andrew. 'I'm just out of work – mind if I grab a slice?'

'Go ahead,' I said.

He bought a slice of pepperoni pizza too. I started off by asking them the usual questions – was Kayla in a good mood? Did she mention if anything was wrong? Did they notice anything suspicious? They had the same answers as her sisters and Ellie – she was in a great mood, having lots of fun, just like everybody else. Andrew finished his slice within a few minutes, but Amy didn't touch hers. She tore off a piece, but didn't put it near her mouth, instead dropping it down on the plate. I had a lot of sympathy for her. I knew I wouldn't be able to stomach a pizza if I were sitting next to Cian.

It felt like I wasn't making much progress though, like the stuff I was hearing was the same from everybody. At least one person from the group had to be lying, or knew things but wasn't telling me. But the answers that Andrew and Amy and the others had given me corresponded exactly with their statements and with what they'd told the police. I suppose it didn't matter so much what they told me, but what I picked up did matter. I was meant to be able to see beyond any lies and cover-ups and find out what really happened.

'We should get going,' said Amy, dumping her slice of pizza into the bin. 'Before it gets too late.'

We walked up the hill, past the tram tracks and down to Kayla's house. There was a blue Mini parked in the driveway, giant furry dice hanging from the rear-view mirror. The lights were on in the sitting room and I could hear loud music coming from inside.

'That's Hazel's car,' said Andrew. 'It was parked in that exact spot on the night of the party, along with some other cars. Amy and I walked over from my house, and got here about nine p.m. By that stage nearly everybody else was here.'

'How close are you to Kayla?' I asked Amy.

'Very close,' said Amy. 'She's one of my best friends.'

Amy didn't act like Libby or Ellie; she didn't look like she was going to cry when she talked about Kayla. Instead she had a sort of vacant expression on her face, like her mind was somewhere else. It must have been hard to know that so many people partly blamed her for what happened to Kayla. I wondered what had been going through her head when she'd left her at the top of the road. I was wary of accusing her of leaving Kayla – I didn't want her to become even more closed off.

'So, you guys left the house at about twelve thirty a.m.?' I asked.

'Yeah,' said Andrew. 'Amy and Kayla wanted to go buy marshmallows, and I said I'd go with them.'

'Because you didn't think they should go alone?' I asked.

'No, I needed cigarettes and fancied a walk.'

I'd thought maybe he'd been concerned for their safety, but obviously not.

'Always the gentleman,' muttered Amy and rolled her eyes. 'Anyway, it was Kayla's idea,' she continued. 'We started talking about this time we'd gone camping and toasted marshmallows, and then Kayla said we should go buy some. The next thing I knew we were heading to the shop.'

'We walked pretty fast,' said Andrew, leading us up the path. 'None of us had drunk that much.'

'While you were walking to the shop, did you notice anything suspicious?' I asked.

'No,' Andrew responded. 'Like I said, everything seemed normal. Kayla was being kind of quiet, but Amy said that's what she's like anyway, so I didn't think much of it at the time.'

I looked round at Amy; she hadn't said anything at all on the walk. She stayed a short distance behind us.

'Is this how you remember it too?' I asked. She just nodded. It must have been a particularly messy break-up or else this journey was particularly difficult for her.

'So, we crossed the road here,' said Andrew. 'Then went this way.'

We were on a busier road now and I could see the mini-supermarket up ahead, its OPEN 24 HOURS sign shining brightly.

Andrew crossed the path and walked ahead of us.

'Did she talk at all?' I said. 'On the walk?'

'Oh yeah, she talked about the party, and all the presents she'd got so far, that sort of stuff.'

'Did she mention a fight with anyone?'

'No, she didn't talk about anything like that,' said Andrew.

I felt like I wasn't making much progress at all.

'Did you notice anyone hanging around on the way up?' I asked, desperate for some new information.

'Nope. We passed a man walking a dog here, then we crossed at these traffic lights.' Andrew hit the pedestrian button. It turned green almost immediately. 'We crossed the road and arrived at another set of lights. We didn't have to wait for these to change, just like now, because there was no traffic.'

It was so strange to walk like this, hearing Andrew recount every detail. It was like I could see it all unfolding in front of me. Kayla had walked this path, completely oblivious to what was about to happen. I wanted to go back in time and tell her to turn round.

Andrew walked into the shop and Amy and I followed. It was a small supermarket, with two cashiers. 'Marshmallows were down the back somewhere,' he said. 'I waited here while the girls went and got them.'

The next part was the one I was most interested in, the part where they left Kayla alone.

We walked back the way we'd come. This time Amy took the lead, staring straight ahead and not looking at either of us as she talked.

'We always stopped here,' said Amy. 'I always left her here.' We were at the top of Kayla's street.

I looked down the road. You could see Kayla's house from where we were standing. It wasn't very far away at all. This made me think that maybe someone was waiting for her, someone from the party who had been holding out until she was alone.

When I got home I looked at the video from the party again. I'd told Amy and Andrew that they could go after we'd walked back from the shop – there wasn't much more I could ask from them at this stage. They'd left separately without even a word of goodbye to each other. Sitting on my bed and watching the video on my laptop, over and over, they seemed like a different couple, standing together, hands entwined, and I thought about how much could change over such a short time.

I scanned the rest of the people in the semicircle that had formed round Kayla's chair. I could see Ellie, wearing a pretty purple strapless dress, her hair tied up in a loose ponytail. And Libby was there too, smiling broadly. She had her arm round a guy, presumably her boyfriend Rob, whose name had been scratched off the list. He was a really good-looking guy, exactly the kind I'd expect Libby to go for. Amy watched as Andrew went up to kiss Kayla on the cheek. Another guy, who was tall and skinny, went up after him. He kissed her on the lips and she smiled. I looked carefully at the crowd, searching for anything suspicious, but nothing jumped out at me. I heard somebody shout 'Fifteen!' and then Hazel gave Kayla a quick kiss on the lips. A guy wolf-whistled and then walked up to Kayla. He kissed her on the lips too. This time she didn't smile though. He leaned in, and I couldn't hear it, but I was sure he whispered something in her ear. I rewound the video and it definitely seemed like he had whispered something to her. He didn't get to say much though because another guy playfully pushed him away and gave Kayla her eighteenth and final kiss.

Chapter 11

I was grateful that *Electric* gave us an hour lunch break: it meant that I could gather my thoughts together and review what I'd learned about Kayla over the last couple of days. I bought some mint ice cream from the ice-cream shop on the square. I loved the ice-cream place. All its tables were outside on Temple Bar Square, so it was a great place to people-watch. They served their ice cream in blue tubs with colourful plastic spoons. I always got sprinkles. They made my mint ice cream look like a tiny rainbow had exploded into millions of pieces on top of it. When Hannah and I were younger, my dad would often bring us here on Saturdays. If we got cones, he'd always manage to talk the lady who was working there into giving him two flakes. Everybody loved my dad. Being back here, I was beginning to understand why Mum had wanted to move. There were reminders of Dad everywhere in this city, from the places we used to go, to the things he liked. Mostly I found it comforting, but I could see why Mum needed to start a new life.

I sat down outside and took out my notebook, forcing myself to stop thinking about the past and instead focus on everything I'd learned about Kayla and the people who knew her. I wrote down all the important things so far, like the last time each of the people had seen Kayla, what they thought had happened and what their relationships were to each other. I'd only talked to five of the eight possible suspects, and already I had tons to consider.

'Ice cream for lunch! I like your style, Jacki King.'

I looked up, surprised to see Dillon standing there. He had rushed off as soon as lunch break came. I'd been shelving stuff in the archive and saw him practically run out of the office. I thought he was going to meet Maggie. There were still unconfirmed rumours that they were going out, but Hannah didn't have very high hopes for them. Apparently Mark had told her that Dillon hardly ever stayed with the same girl for more than two weeks, that he hardly ever went out with anyone in fact. He didn't seem to be a girlfriend type of guy.

He sat down across from me, putting a yellow bag he'd been holding on the ground beside him and picked up the ice-cream menu.

'I was in Tower Records,' he said. 'The new Mighty Stef single is out today. There were signed copies for the first one hundred people.'

'You ran to Tower Records to get the new Mighty Stef single?'

'Is that crazy?' he said.

'Impressive,' I said with a smile.

'You like the Mighty Stef?' he asked.

'Love him.'

'I thought you would,' he said. 'When you were in Ellie's

office the other day I heard one of the guys say he might be the special guest at the Unsigned gig, although it's not confirmed. What did she want you for anyway?' he added, pulling the record out of the bag.

'Oh, she just wanted me to address invitations,' I said. 'Nothing important.'

Sometimes I surprised myself at how quickly I was able to lie now, how fast the lies came to me.

He held the record out to me and I examined it.

'It looks deadly,' I said. 'I really like the artwork.'

I handed it back to him.

'That one's yours,' he said.

'What?'

'I got you one too.'

'Why?'

Dillon blushed.

'I mean . . . thanks!' I said. 'This is really cool.'

'No problem,' he said.

I told myself he'd just bought it for me as a friend. I mean, I got Colin stuff all the time. But I also knew this wasn't something I would share with Nick – he probably wouldn't understand and things weren't great between us at the moment. I'd talked to him last night on the phone; I'd asked him was he excited about the gig and he'd gone kind of quiet. I'd decided that once I got back to Avarna, I was going to tell him everything – why I was really in Dublin and exactly what had happened last summer. My secrets were definitely coming between us. I really hoped he'd understand.

Sensing that Dillon felt the tension of the moment as much as I did, I hastily moved the conversation on. 'So, what's your favourite Stef song?' I asked. 'Mine's "Prayer for the Broken Hearted".'

We chatted for ages again, sticking to safe subjects like music, and before we knew it, it was five to two. It didn't help that Dillon had hilariously deliberated for ages about which ice-cream flavour to get.

We rushed back to St Stephen's Green, weaving through all the people as fast as we could. The traffic lights were taking ages to change and Dillon shuffled nervously. 'Come on,' he said, then grabbed my hand and pulled me across the road.

I felt my heart beating a little bit faster than it should.

Chapter 12

The next person on my list was Calum. I met him straight after work. I'd watched the video of the party again on my laptop, more carefully this time, and was now positive that I'd seen him whisper something in Kayla's ear. I was determined to find out what it was.

'I've already told the police everything I know,' said Calum. He wore faded denims and a rugby shirt, so tight that it clung to the muscles on his arms. He was sitting across from me at one of the tables in Rage, eating the fries Hazel had given him. She'd gone back behind the bar so it was just him and me again, and I was finding him kind of painful to listen to. 'I mean, you sleep with a girl and suddenly you're a prime suspect.'

It was obvious he didn't want to be here. He was one of the most annoying guys I'd ever met. He was being very defensive and I suspected he was hiding something.

'I'm not here to make your life difficult, I just want to find Kayla,' I said. 'You want that too, right?'

'Yes.'

'Well then, let's talk.'

'OK, if you insist,' he said with a sigh. 'Basically, Kayla

and me, we broke up about a month before the party. We hadn't been going out very long – about nine days, I'd say – but what annoyed me most was that she denied going out with me at all. I don't know why, but she did. Of course I told people we'd been going out because the best thing about sleeping with Kayla Edwards is that you get to tell people about it . . .'

I felt my stomach twist in disgust, but let him carry on.

'She still denied it. Everybody was calling *me* a liar. I don't know why she was doing it; maybe she wanted to get back at me because I hadn't, I dunno, treated her right or whatever. So yeah, I was pretty pissed off. I didn't want to hurt the girl, I just wanted her to admit that she'd slept with me.'

'Did you ever think maybe she wanted to keep it private?'

'Listen, Jacki . . . that's your name, right, Jacki? This wasn't some sort of delicate love affair that she wanted to keep secret, locked between us forever. She came over to my house one night and basically said we should get together. I'd seen this before – somebody trying to get back at their boyfriend – and I was happy to oblige. If some guy messes up, that's his problem, not mine. And this was Kayla Edwards. Arriving at my door, basically offering herself to me. It was like something out of a dream. Sure, she seems a bit messed up in the head, but she is also seriously hot. And it's not like she asked me not to tell anybody. I assumed she wanted to get back at someone, but she didn't tell me who it was, and she didn't tell me not to tell. So I mentioned it to one of the lads, and gossip spreads here like you wouldn't believe. But she denied it. Acted like it had never even happened. Like I'd made the whole thing up. And I'm known to exaggerate so, needless to say, nobody believed me. So, yeah, I was pissed off at her. I was pissed off at her the night she went missing. But I didn't *kill* her.'

I didn't like Calum at all, but in a weird way, he actually seemed honest. Either that or he was a really good liar.

'Why were you at her birthday party?' I asked. 'If you were so pissed off with her?'

'She lives right across the road from me, so I thought why not? I'm really good mates with Libby, and plus – free booze and hot girls . . . I was hardly going to pass that up.'

'What did you whisper to her?' I asked. 'In the video. What did you whisper in her ear?'

'I can't tell you that,' he said. 'I didn't have to tell you any of this. Look, I didn't kill her, I didn't hurt her, I didn't touch her. At least not anywhere she didn't want me to. Listen, I gotta go . . . I need to get to practice,' he said. And then he was gone.

Hazel came over to the table, bringing me a Coke, even though I hadn't asked for one.

'Hey,' she said. 'This is on the house.'

'Thanks,' I said.

She gave me a sympathetic smile. 'I know he's not the most polite person on the planet, but he's a good friend. I don't want to interfere, but I just wanted to say, don't let him upset you. He's like that with everyone – I think he wants to keep a tough-guy image. He was really shaken by Kayla's disappearance though; he was so upset about it.'

I wondered if he'd been upset because he was hiding something. But then again, my gut instinct was to think that he was telling the truth.

'I don't think he really wanted to be here,' I said.

'He's just tired of it all,' said Hazel. 'Some people suspect him because he told everyone he slept with Kayla.'

'Do you think he did?' I asked.

'Honestly, I don't know,' said Hazel. 'She's not his type at all, but then again, she didn't really tell me who she was dating, so it's quite possible.'

I felt my phone buzzing in my pocket. There was a text from Nick. It said:

I really miss you. I booked a train ticket to Dublin. Meet me for dinner tomorrow?

I smiled. I was so glad he was coming up. Things had been so weird between us lately – seeing him would hopefully help clear the air.

Of course. I'd love that x, I texted back.

'Was that your boyfriend?' said Hazel, dramatically inflecting the last word.

'Yes,' I said sheepishly.

'What's his name?' she asked.

'Nick.'

'Is he hot?'

I laughed. 'Yes.'

'Nice work.'

'Do you have a boyfriend?' I asked. I was pretty sure I knew the answer though. I couldn't imagine that somebody like her wouldn't have one.

'Yeah,' she said, 'I do. His name's Barry. I haven't seen him in a couple of weeks though; he's in the army, so he's away a lot.'

I remembered Ellie had mentioned him. She'd said that he'd been manning the door at the party. I guess if you're in the army then you'd make a pretty good bouncer.

'When does he get back?' I asked.

'July,' she said. I thought that must be pretty hard. It made me feel bad for moaning about not seeing Nick that much. At least he was never too far away. And I was so delighted he was coming up to Dublin. Maybe we'd go to a gig or go to the cinema or just hang out, only the two of us. I was starting to make plans when it suddenly hit me. We wouldn't be going to any of those. We were going to see *A Midsummer Night's Dream*. With Special Effects.

'I thought we could do something together,' said Nick. 'Just the two of us.' He'd hardly touched his bacon and cheese fries. I put down my burger and looked out the window on to Dame Street, watching people walk past the diner. The Kinks were playing on the jukebox, my boyfriend was here, we were eating some of the best fast food in town. It should have been fun. And yet, we were fighting. Again.

'I have to go to this play,' I said. 'I told Hannah I'd go, and Colin is coming up for it. I can't not go, she'll kill me.'

'Didn't you go to see her in this before Christmas?' he asked, stabbing his fork into a piece of bacon.

'It's a different production,' I said. 'It's sold out, but I managed to get you a ticket. Come on, it'll be a laugh.'

Nick raised an eyebrow. 'You should have just told me to come up tomorrow instead; I've told the lads I'll practise tomorrow now, so I'll have to go home in the morning.'

'Come on, Nick, I totally forgot, I've been really busy.'

He sighed. 'Right, fine. I'll go to it.'

I felt kind of bad. I'd been so busy that I'd totally forgotten. I wanted to talk to Nick too, and it was so nice of him to come all this way. But I knew if I ditched Hannah's play to hang out with him that I'd never hear the end of it from her. Besides, I was kind of looking forward to it. Sophie and Ross and Colin were all going too.

'At least we'll have a few hours alone before the play,' said Nick.

'Well actually, I . . .'

I didn't need to explain. Nick looked to his right, to see Colin's face pressed up against the restaurant's window. A few seconds later he was inside.

''Sup?' he said, stealing one of Nick's fries. 'Ready for some drama?'

'Hey!' I said. 'How'd your date go?' Colin and James had got on so well on their second date that they'd already gone on a third. I was so glad that it was working out. They looked so cute together – I had high hopes for them and I really wanted to hear all the details.

'Oh yeah, it . . . it went well.'

We exchanged glances. I could tell he was holding back because Nick was there.

I think Nick sensed it too. 'I'm going to the bathroom,' he said, with a roll of his eyes.

'Well?' I said.

Colin scooched in closer to me.

'It was great,' he said. 'We went to an exhibition in Sligo and then for a walk on the beach. It was so nice. But then I just, kind of, you know, jokingly suggested we were, like, a "couple", but James said he didn't want anything serious. Like, he wants to keep it casual.'

'Oh,' I said. 'So he doesn't want a boyfriend?'

'He says he's not big into labels,' Colin explained. 'With his last boyfriend, he says they got serious too soon and that they both just ended up getting hurt. He doesn't want that to happen to us.'

'And you're OK with that?' I asked. I couldn't help but think that this was hurting Colin.

'I told him I was OK with it.'

'But you're not?' I said.

'Of course I'm not!' exclaimed Colin. 'I've never had a boyfriend. I want one – I don't care if I get hurt! Maybe he'll change his mind . . .'

'I dunno,' I said. 'If he says he doesn't want to get serious then –'

Nick came back to the table and Colin started to talk about what dessert he was going to order. I don't think he wanted to talk about it in front of Nick, so I decided to leave any further questioning until later.

'Sophie, can I sit there?' said Ross. 'I want to sit beside Jacki.' People were starting to wander into the auditorium. We were some of the first there, so we'd got really good seats.

'Why?' said Sophie.

'Because I haven't seen her in ages.'

'Neither have I,' said Sophie.

I laughed. 'He wants to sit there in case a hot girl sits next to him,' I explained.

'What?' said Sophie.

'Sophie,' said Ross, standing up straighter as if about to give a lecture. 'This is a Shakespearean play. Which means there is about a seventy-five per cent chance that a female is going to sit in that empty seat next to you. Out of that seventy-five per cent, considering this is a youth theatre production, there's about a forty per cent chance that female will be between fifteen and nineteen years old. Out of that forty per cent, there's a twenty-one per cent chance that girl will be single. That's a chance I'm willing to take.'

'Those statistics are completely wrong,' said Sophie.

'What's wrong,' said Ross, 'is that *you're still sitting in my seat.*'

Sophie sighed and stood up, then shuffled in past Nick and Colin and me. The auditorium was filling up, mostly with friends and family of the cast. I recognized a few of Hannah's friends from drama class, and there were a couple of guys we used to hang out with sitting in the front row. I waved over at them and they waved back.

'I've really missed you,' whispered Nick, playing with the bracelet on my wrist.

'I've missed you too,' I said.

'Shhh,' said a woman in the front row as the curtain rose, and we couldn't say any more.

Sophie, Colin, Ross, Nick and I were standing in a circle when Hannah came skipping across the lobby.

'Well?' she said. 'What did you think?'

'*You* were brilliant,' I said, which was a nice way of saying 'The play kind of sucked, but you didn't.' She was brilliant though – she always is. Hannah wants to do drama at Trinity, and her entire life seems to be devoted to this goal. She gets involved in as many plays as she can manage – her CV must be a hundred pages long at this stage. If she doesn't get in, I'm not sure what she's going to do. Ross has always said he's going to emigrate the day our college offers come out because he's scared of what sort of destruction she'll cause if she doesn't get in.

'I really liked the costumes,' said Colin. He sounded a bit more cheerful than earlier, which was good.

'Did you all get a programme?' asked Hannah.

'Yep,' we said in unison. 'Will you sign mine?' I said, just because I knew she was dying for somebody to ask.

'I think I'm gonna head on,' Nick whispered.

'What?' I couldn't believe he was bailing so early. 'But we're going out after. Can't you stay for another little while? We haven't really had a chance to catch up properly.'

'I'm crashing at my aunt's house and she doesn't like it when I come back too late. Besides, I didn't realize I'd have to come to *this* tonight.'

'Aw, Nick, I'm sorry the evening didn't work out,' I whispered. 'I couldn't wait to see you. But I couldn't *not* go to Hannah's play, she'd have killed me.'

'Back in a sec!' said Hannah. 'I think I see some of the girls from dance class over there.'

'I'm just really tired,' said Nick more loudly.

'Jesus, Nick, would you ever man up,' said Colin jokingly.

'What?' said Nick.

'C'mon, stop moaning.'

'Will you just stay out of this,' said Nick. 'I'm going,' he added, turning to me. 'I'll call you tomorrow.' He kissed me quickly on the cheek and walked out of the theatre. I couldn't believe what had just happened. I looked at the others, who all seemed equally stunned. I ran after him, but he was already out of sight by the time I'd pushed my way through the crowd. I couldn't hold back the tears; I was so upset that he'd just left like that.

Colin came out after me.

'Why did you have to say that?' I asked. 'He was already in a bad mood; you've just gone and made it worse.'

'Why are you even still with him?' said Colin. 'How the hell do you listen to that?'

'You can't choose who you love, Colin. Your heart chooses it.'

'Well, tell your heart to catch up with your head. You can choose when to let go of them. And you need to cut that loose, Jacki, because he's not treating you right.'

'How dare you say that!' I was getting angrier by the second. 'You're just jealous because you've never had a proper boyfriend.' The moment I'd said it I wished I could reach into the air and snatch it back, but it was out there now, and I saw Colin's reaction. He was really hurt.

'Oh yeah, I'm so jealous that I don't get to stand in Temple Bar with mascara smeared down my face, running after some guy in a Ramones T-shirt with crap hair and an even crappier band.'

'Why do you hate him so much?'

'I don't hate him, I love you! And I can't stand watching you get walked all over by him. The others are happy to stand on the sidelines and nod and smile while you make excuses for him, but I'm not. You have to wake up!'

'I don't understand why you're being so horrible to me.'

'I'm not the one being horrible to you, Jacki. Call me when you cop on to that.'

Colin stormed off in the same direction as Nick, and I was left standing there, alone.

Chapter 13

The next day I went into a coffee shop in town to meet another person who'd been at the party – Sasha Finnigan. She had an alibi, but had heard about me from Ellie and wanted to help in any way she could, so I decided to meet with her. I figured it would do no harm to hear about the party from somebody who wasn't a suspect. I tried to forget about last night, to concentrate on the case and get the image of the hurt look on Colin's face out of my head. And, most of all, I tried to forget how angry I was at Nick.

We'd arranged to meet in the coffee shop in Tower Records, one of my favourite places in the entire universe. I was early so I had a look at the EPs on sale down the back of the shop. I really wanted a turntable. I had an old record player that had belonged to my dad, but it was very temperamental and didn't always work. That didn't stop me buying records though. I saw lots that I wanted, but I was trying to save some money to buy a new amp, so didn't make any purchases. I also had a look in the book section and flicked through Bob Dylan's *Chronicles* until it was four thirty and time to meet Sasha.

When I went upstairs, she was already sitting at one of

the tables. The coffee shop was decorated with mismatched furniture and had a 70s vibe. The milk was in glass bottles on the tables and the armchairs were like something you'd expect to find in your grandparents' back room. On the ceiling there were framed posters of classic movies, and stacks of film magazines were scattered about.

'Hi, Sasha,' I said. 'I'm Jacki.'

'Hey,' replied Sasha, giving me a welcoming smile 'It's nice to meet you.'

'Can I get you something?' I offered.

'Oh, yes, please, I'll have a chai latte,' she said.

'OK,' I said. 'I'll be back in a second.'

'How long have you known Kayla?' I asked, after the lady had brought us our drinks.

'Since first year,' said Sasha. 'We ended up in the same class, and we've had the same group of friends since then. I'm not as close to her as some of the others, like Kev and Amy, but I know her really well.'

'How would you describe her?'

'Enigmatic,' she said. 'But not in a stand-offish way. It just makes you want to get to know her even more. She's also unbelievably pretty. Probably the prettiest girl in our year, after Libby. But she's different pretty to Libby. Libby is always immaculately put together, whereas Kayla is just effortlessly beautiful . . . but don't tell Libby I said that.' She laughed nervously.

'I won't,' I said with a smile.

'Was Kayla dating anyone?' I asked. 'That you know of.'

'I hadn't heard of her dating anyone since Kev. I think

that break-up really hit her hard, even though she was the one to end it. He just pushed her too far. It came out later that she was actually seeing Luke, although none of us knew. She was a fairly secretive person – she didn't reveal too much of herself.'

I nodded. I understood that, considering there were only a few people who I was really open with.

'How is her relationship with Amy?' I asked.

'They're best friends and never really fight – only about one thing. Everybody knows that Andrew was obsessed with Kayla, like, for years. Kayla didn't fancy him, but they ended up hooking up one night at a party. It never went any further though. Amy knew about all of this, of course. And she acted like it didn't matter at first, but she's kind of insecure, and she was jealous that Andrew and Kayla had this history. She was doing so well too, but then one night Andrew called her Kayla by mistake. In front of everyone. And she just flipped. I guess she'd been holding it inside for so long that it all came out there and then. Of course Kayla had no idea that Amy felt like this. Things were weird between them for a while, but then they were fine again. Kayla kind of kept her distance from Andrew, stopped going to stuff alone with him and all that. But, like I say, that was the only thing they ever fought about.'

Andrew hadn't mentioned that he'd liked Kayla, but I suppose he wouldn't, not in front of Amy. This gave me a reason to be suspicious of him. If he'd been obsessed with her for years, then maybe he was still obsessed with her the night of the party. Maybe he was jealous that she'd found happiness with somebody else. Maybe he was jealous of

Luke, or if he didn't know about them then Calum, perhaps?

'What about Calum,' I said. 'Was there anything going on with him?'

'I can't believe he's still claiming she slept with him,' said Sasha. 'You couldn't get any further from her type than Calum, he's such a sleaze. He's been with over eighty per cent of the girls in our year. She would *not* have gone for him.'

I was surprised Sasha was so convinced. I'd felt that Calum was telling the truth.

'Was Kev still upset about the break-up?' I asked.

'Yeah, definitely. Did you hear that there were twenty-five calls to her in his call history? Basically, every night there would be twenty-five missed calls. I know he was upset and everything, but he had stepped over into stalker territory. I know everybody says, *Oh, he's so nice*, but I used to go out with him and I've seen how angry he can get. You wouldn't think it, but if he gets pissed off he gets, like, seriously scary. I was having a fight with him once and he hit the windscreen of my car so hard with his fist, I had to pull over and tell him to get the hell out. I broke up with him the next day and I've hardly talked to him since. Everybody thinks I was being dramatic, but I was actually scared, like, properly terrified of him at that moment. I'm not saying he would do anything, but I'm just saying I wouldn't be surprised if she was scared too.'

I hadn't met Kev yet, but twenty-five missed calls did seem excessive.

'When did you first hear she was missing?' I asked.

'The next morning,' said Sasha. 'I was really hungover – I think we all were – but everybody was out, determined to find her. It was about the ninth and tenth day when people started dropping off – those are the days that nobody likes to talk about. They had to get back to their own lives, but some of us were still looking. By the next weekend even we couldn't keep doing it – work wouldn't let me take any more time off. Amy and Andrew went home because I don't think they could hack it any more. Everyone was tired and frustrated and they started to turn on them. And it was sixth year, it was February and we had to study for our mocks. We couldn't keep looking for her.'

'Do you remember anything odd at the party?' I asked.

'I remember Barry being in a really bad mood,' said Sasha. 'I don't know what was wrong with him. Maybe he was stressed because he was responsible for keeping the party under control. And Libby was a bit off, but I think that's just because she was worried about the house; you can never really relax when it's in your gaff. Also, people were kind of annoyed that there was only one toilet, which someone had got sick in. There was a sign at the bottom of the stairs saying upstairs was strictly out of bounds, and Barry wouldn't let anyone go up there, even though the downstairs bathroom was, like, disgusting.'

'Do you remember anything else?'

'Honestly . . . no,' she said. 'It wasn't till the next morning when I got a call from Hazel that I realized something was wrong. The poor girl, she sounded so upset . . .'

'Oh, crap,' said Sasha, looking at the clock. 'I have to head back to work. They're really strict in my place. But I

live just up on Dame Street, with Ellie, actually; you're working on her magazine, right?'

'Yeah,' I said.

'Well, if you need to talk to me again I'm around town
most of the time.'

'Thanks, Sasha,' I said.

The next name on my list was Kev. I was due to meet him
later today in the shop where he worked. And now, after
everything Sasha had told me, I really hoped there would
be other people there too.

Chapter 14

The charity bookshop was definitely the coolest I'd ever seen. The shelves were hot pink and baby blue, and there was a table with boxes of records inside the door, all priced at one euro. There was a girl arranging a display of detective novels in the centre of the shop, trying to get a battered copy of *The Big Sleep* to stand upright. She smiled at me, then turned her attention to the display. There was a guy sitting on a high stool behind the till, with brown hair and glasses. He looked exactly like he did in the video.

A young woman arrived at the counter with a stack of paperbacks, so I browsed the shelves for a few minutes, stopping at the memoirs. They were mainly ones of politicians and reality TV stars, but I spotted a PJ Harvey squashed in between two Hitler biographies. I made a mental note to buy it on the way out.

'Hey,' he said, and that's when I realized he was standing right behind me.

'Hey,' I said, turning to face him. 'I'm Jacki.'

'Oh yeah . . . sorry, I'm Kevin. Although you probably already knew that.'

I nodded. 'Can I talk to you for a few minutes?'

He opened the door that led to the back room. It was filled with books – all sorted into different piles. We sat down at the table and Kev pushed some stuff aside – price stickers and a pair of scissors.

'Would you like tea?' he said, pointing to the giant box of fair trade teabags over on the table.

'Oh, no thanks,' I said.

'You sure?'

'Yeah, I better get started.'

Kev was definitely the most on edge of all the people I'd talked to so far – he even rivalled Calum. He crossed his arms, uncrossed them, then crossed them again. I thought it best to just dive straight in, no point in tiptoeing about.

'I heard there were twenty-five missed calls on Kayla's phone from you the next morning,' I told him. 'Were you worried about her?'

'I just wanted to apologize,' he said. 'I wanted to make things right. I should never have gone to her birthday party. But I just thought if I brought her that really nice present and told her how sorry I was then she'd forgive me and everything would be OK. I mean, you'll do anything to make the hurt stop. I sat on my bed and just kept dialling her number until she picked up. I knew she would eventually because you can make somebody so angry that they will pick up just to shout at you. And I know it makes no sense, but even that little bit of contact eased the pain, just for a second. Even though she was screaming at me to leave her alone, when I hung up I was happier because I loved her so much that at that point I'd rather fight with her than talk to any other girl. I loved everything about her. But the night of the party though . . . she didn't pick up.

'Nobody told me she was seeing that other guy. You think your friends would tell you something like that, but nobody bothered to say it to me!'

Kev sounded pretty desperate – desperate enough to hurt Kayla? I wasn't sure, but then again love does cloud your judgement – maybe he'd been too emotional to think straight.

'So nobody told you about Luke?' I said.

'No. I walked in on them in her bedroom and I freaked out. I called her a slut and all this other horrible stuff, which I should never have done; we'd broken up – she was perfectly entitled to be with whoever she wanted. But, seeing the two of them on her bed, I just flipped. The next morning I woke up and remembered all the stuff I'd said, and I just needed to make it right. I was so afraid that I'd ruined any chance of us ever being friends again, and I couldn't bear that, so I needed to fix it. But she wouldn't answer her phone. I figured she was just mad, and if I called enough times then she'd eventually give in and pick up. But she didn't.'

'Did you crash the party?' I'd thought nobody had been able to get past Barry.

'No, I'd been invited . . . but when we broke up nobody expected me to actually come. But it's not like she asked me to stay away or anything; I know I probably should have stayed at home, but I really thought she still loved me and that she was just angry. I wasn't prepared for the indifference. She didn't love me any more. I had a feeling Luke liked her. I saw them talking online all the time, but I didn't think she liked him in that way.'

'So you were stalking her?'

'Oh, come on, don't tell me you've never done it?'

I didn't answer. I scanned the room, with its stacks of spineless books ready to be discarded. Kev crossed and uncrossed his arms again. Sitting with him was making me anxious.

'I'd seen the way he looked at her,' he said, narrowing his eyes. 'The same way I did. I knew there was something going on, but I thought she was doing it to make me jealous, or to numb the pain. I didn't think she was actually in love with him. He didn't appreciate her. He wasn't right for her. His friends are all crazy and into drugs and she's just not like that. I don't think he's good enough for her.'

I was starting to feel really uncomfortable. Kev sounded so angry. But I had some more questions for him, so I had to stay.

'What happened then?' I said. 'After you walked in on them.'

'She told me to follow her and then led me into one of the other rooms and talked to me for a few minutes. I don't remember what she said. All I remember is the indifference. In her voice, in her eyes. She didn't love me any more. She was infatuated with him. I'd got it wrong. I'd convinced myself it was just because she was mad and she wanted to make me suffer. But as she talked I realized that it wasn't because of that and she didn't just want to hurt me. She really liked him and she'd probably really liked him for a while – and that hurt more than anything else.'

'Did that make you angry?' I asked. I couldn't imagine him taking something like that very well.

'No . . . I was upset. I didn't even apologize for saying all those things. I was so upset that I just turned round and walked away, down the stairs and out the door and just kept walking.'

'Where did you go?' I asked. I'd read in his statement that he'd started walking, but wasn't sure where he'd gone. I found that kind of unbelievable.

'I don't really want to say,' he said, looking down at the table, gripping the handle of his cup, but not moving it.

'Why?' I asked.

'It's embarrassing,' he said, clenching his hand tighter.

'More embarrassing than ending up in jail?'

'OK, fine,' he said, looking at me. 'Don't tell anyone this . . . but I sat on the ground behind the sports hall and cried. A few of my mates were down at the school drinking, and I was going there to meet them, but on the way I just sort of collapsed. I didn't take any notice of what was going on around me because my face was buried in my hands. Then I got up and met my friends and acted like everything was fine. Because that's what you have to do – you just act like everything is OK.'

Chapter 15

George's Street Arcade was pretty busy. Loads of people were browsing the stalls. I walked down the aisle filled with *Hello Kitty* merchandise, where you could get anything you wanted with *Hello Kitty* on it – from trainers to wallets to phones. After that was a stall with multicoloured tights and bowler hats and fairy wings. Next there were tables with manga and anime merchandise, comics and superhero action figures; you could also buy records or rare books or vintage dresses or powdery pink Turkish delight. The arcade was a wonderful mix of knick-knacks and clothes and sweets.

I could see the fortune-teller sign up ahead, a painting of an old woman holding a crystal ball, with silver and gold swirls coming out of it. I arrived at the stall, pulled back the purple velvet curtain and stepped inside. Lauren was sitting there, with a book open in front of her.

'Oh, hey,' she said. 'Jacki, right?'

She was wearing a green silk shawl, which gave her a mystical look. Her brown hair was tied up in a bun. She was also wearing big gold hoop earrings and lots of bracelets.

'Hi,' I said. 'Thanks for seeing me today. I know you're really busy.'

'Yeah, sure, have a seat,' she said. 'I know, it's crazy busy these days, lots of people wanting to know their futures. I'll have my student loan paid off in no time if things keep going the way they are.'

'What are you studying?' I asked.

'Commercial Law,' she said. 'I'm in my final year. This is really handy because I get to pick my own hours and the money is pretty good.'

'How much do you charge, if you don't mind me asking?'

'Sixty euro a session,' she said. 'That's for about half an hour.'

'Wow.'

'You should start doing it yourself,' she said. 'If you've got any sort of psychic ability, then you should give it a try.'

I laughed. I didn't think it was my sort of thing.

'So, you want to ask me about the party?' she said.

'Yeah,' I replied. 'Do you remember much about it?'

'I got there kind of late because I was waiting on my dad to get home so he could give me a lift. I'd got Kayla this really cool fake fish-tank thing to hang on her wall, but it was super-heavy so I couldn't bring it on the bus. I got there and the party was packed already. I knew most of the people there, but not everyone. I was in Kayla's year, but not in her class. I knew her really well from camera club though, and also through Hazel because I used to work at Rage at weekends. I went home pretty early too because my parents are super-strict about studying, and we had the mocks coming up. I was out of there by twelve thirty. So I'm not much help, I'm afraid.'

'Do you remember noticing anything . . . now, looking back on it?'

'No, I can't really remember much at all; it's all kind of a blur. You know when you're not consciously observing stuff things just slip past you? I couldn't even tell you what most of the people were wearing. I'm not even sure what I was wearing. It's weird.'

'Did you know Kayla was seeing Luke?'

'No, she kept that one quiet! She probably wouldn't have told me anyway. We weren't that close, but I'm surprised Amy didn't know. Although I think Kayla kept it quiet because she didn't want Kev to find out. I think she still really cared for him, even though she didn't want to be with him any more. Although that's just my opinion. I'm not really sure.'

'Thanks,' I said.

'Sorry I couldn't really be more help.'

'No, it's fine. Anything at all that you can tell me is great.'

'So tell me, Jacki,' she said. 'Do you think Kayla's dead?'

'You must know already,' I said. 'If you're a fortune-teller? You must know if she's coming back or not.'

'I tell people I don't know,' she said. 'But you're right, yeah, I have a feeling. I just hope I'm wrong.'

She must have suspected that Kayla was dead too, I thought.

'Am I wrong?' she asked, her voice quivering.

'I probably shouldn't discuss details of the case,' I said, 'without checking with Detective Sergeant Lawlor if it's OK.'

'Oh, of course,' she said, but she could probably guess what I meant by that.

'I suppose I better get going,' I said.

'I have some time before my next appointment,' said Lauren. 'Want me to read your fortune?'

I hesitated again, but then thought, *What the hell, why not?* My life couldn't possibly get any weirder.

'Maybe . . .' I said. 'How does it work?'

'Well, I read palms,' said Lauren. 'I learned it from my grandmother. I can tell what's going to happen to people by examining the lines on their hand.'

'OK,' I said. I held out my left hand.

'You're going to go through change soon,' said Lauren. 'It's going to be difficult at first, but it will work out for the best in the end. And you're going to travel, somewhere far away. And you're going to . . .'

Her predictions were all pretty vague. As I walked back to Gran's, I thought about what she'd told me, but couldn't see any major revelations.

When I got home, I read some more of the book Ger had given me. I flicked to the middle pages.

Methods of Psychic Protection

For additional protection, pick an object that you feel represents security and well-being for you, and wear it every day. When you see the object, think of the peace it gives you. Remember to keep it with you at all times, as a symbol of safety.

I found the guitar bracelet Nick had given me and put it on. Like Ger had said, it was better to be prepared.

Chapter 16

The *Electric Unsigned* gig got off to a fairly shaky start. Rage looked great – Ellie had decorated the place really well. The entire ceiling was covered with fairy lights, which made the bar look even more magical than before. There was a projector in the corner, beaming up images of *Electric* magazine covers on to the back wall. There was a slight problem though, as one of the acts had pulled out at the last second.

'What the hell are we going to do?' said Ellie. 'They were meant to be on in an hour; how are we going to get somebody to replace them in an hour?'

'Can you not call somebody?' said Michael. 'Like one of your friends' bands? Ask them to step in?'

'This is meant to be the best of Dublin's unsigned,' said Tim. Ellie looked even more anxious now that her editor had joined the circle. 'There are invited industry professionals here – we have a reputation to uphold.'

'Yes, I understand that,' said Ellie. 'But we need to fill the slot.'

'Can you find a solo artist?' said Tim. 'It would be the least hassle.'

'Jacki's a solo artist,' said Dillon, smiling brightly and nudging me with his elbow.

'Do you write your own stuff?' asked Ellie.

'Yeah,' I said.

'Cos each act tonight is doing one cover, but they also have to sing their own stuff.'

'Hold on,' said Tim. 'I think I've seen you play before. Were you upstairs in Whelan's last week?'

'Yeah,' I said. 'I was.'

'You've found your replacement, Ellie,' said Tim. 'You're on at nine.'

I didn't have time to feel nervous or excited, except about using a strange guitar. I had this thing about always using my own; I felt like I was jinxing my performance by using somebody else's. But there was nothing I could do about it now, so I'd just have to get over it. I don't think I've ever had somebody hug me as hard as Ellie did.

I wasn't on for another hour though, and in the meantime I had to help out, taking money from people at the door, showing the bands to the dressing room, making sure there were bottles of water on stage – that sort of thing. Hazel waved at me from behind the bar. She was wearing a ripped black tank top instead of the orange *Electric Unsigned* T-shirts that the rest of the people working in Rage that night had to wear. I guess when you're assistant manager you don't have to look ridiculous.

It wouldn't have been that bad if I hadn't also been concentrating on the people in the corner. Libby's boyfriend Rob was here, along with Andrew and a very drunk Calum. Every time I walked past them they tried to engage me in conversation.

'So, psychic girl!' said Calum. 'Can you tell me something about my future?'

'What do you want to know?' I said with a sigh.

'Um . . . when am I gonna get laid next?' he said with a laugh, then turned round to Rob and gave him a high-five.

'I can't see *that* far into the future,' I muttered, picking up the empty glasses behind them.

'OOOH!' said Rob and Andrew as I walked off.

I decided to distract myself from Calum's ridiculous comments by seeing if I could pick up any vibes from people in the room who had known Kayla. Things were starting to slow down a bit as far as any new information on Kayla was concerned and I hadn't really got any clues in a while. I decided it was probably best that I carry her necklace with me to really tune in to what was going on around me – there was no point having it if I just left it in my bag all the time. I entered the dressing room and looked in my bag for it, but to my horror, it wasn't there.

'Shit,' I said. 'Shit, shit, shit.' I searched all round the dressing room, hoping it had just fallen out of my bag and that nobody had taken it. That would be terrible. How would I explain to Libby that I'd lost her sister's necklace? I got down on my hands and knees and searched the floor, but there was no sign of it.

'Looking for this?' said Hazel, walking in and holding up the necklace and staring at me disapprovingly.

'Oh, thank god, where was it?'

'On the floor, in the bathrooms,' she said.

'Thanks so much, Hazel,' I said, reaching out and taking it from her. 'I'll take better care of it from now on, I promise.'

'OK,' she said, her anger seeming to fade. 'Andrew left his phone in the toilets too,' she said. 'What is it with you people? Will you give it to him? I have to go find Ellie.'

'Yeah, sure,' I said.

I looked at the phone in my hand and a thought suddenly occurred to me. Could I quickly check it? It did seem kind of bad to go through somebody's phone, but I really wanted to know if he was hiding something, and I couldn't pass this chance up.

I waited until Hazel left and quickly scrolled through his messages, mostly boring ones about rugby practice and ones with tons of kisses from some girl called Kate. If he was going to text something really private, he'd probably delete it afterwards anyway, so maybe this was a waste of time. I checked his email: nothing there either. He should really password-protect his phone, I thought. I was able to access everything. I decided to have a quick look through his photos: more rugby pictures, pictures of girls. Then, to my complete shock, I saw a picture of Kayla, wearing a jersey and boxer shorts and smiling seductively into the camera. I sent the picture to myself, deleted the sent message and then walked back out into the club and returned the phone to Andrew.

I swallowed down a strange sick feeling that had come over me. It must have been guilt from checking Andrew's phone – it's not something I ever would have done before. I was so different from the person I used to know.

Chapter 17

I walked up on to the stage. I was feeling a bit nervous, which was unusual for me. Maybe it was because I knew how important this gig was to everybody at *Electric*, and also because I had to follow a really great folk singer – a guy called Ciaran, who was unbelievably talented. Nevertheless, I approached the mic with pretend confidence. I never really hear anything when I'm performing – I don't notice the crowd talking or anything like that, I just focus on the song. I sang an original, the one I'd sung to Colin in my bedroom, and it got a pretty good response. Ellie gave me the thumbs up from the side of the stage and I was glad I'd made her happy. But I had no idea what cover I was going to play. The seconds ticked by and I tried to think of something. I'd had a few ideas before I got up on stage, but now my mind was just completely blank. *What the hell was I going to sing?* Faces from the crowd looked at me expectantly and I started to panic. Then I saw Nick walking into the room, and I got even more distracted. I was glad he'd come – I wasn't sure if he was going to turn up after the fight we'd had.

'Jacki,' whispered Ellie, and then she shot me a look as

if to say, *What the hell are you doing?* A camera flash blinded me for a second, but instead of making things worse, it helped me snap out of it. I knew what I was going to sing: 'Pictures of You' – the Cure song I'd been listening to every night in my dreams. I'd been thinking about doing my own version, and although I hadn't even practised it properly, I decided it was perfect. I took a deep breath and sang, completely escaping into the world of the song, only to be brought back to the moment by the huge applause I got when I sang the last line.

The buzz I felt from performing was, as always, amazing. It was a feeling that I didn't think could be beaten. I looked at my watch. How was it half ten already? Nick had to go soon and I'd hardly spoken to him all night. I knew this would make him grumpy, but hopefully he'd understand. It's not like *he* hadn't done this kind of thing before, and at least I had a proper excuse. He surely couldn't hold this against me. I hurried out from behind the bar, determined to find him, promising myself I wouldn't get pulled away from his side again tonight, no matter what happened.

I elbowed and nudged my way through the crowd, right up to the stage where the last band was playing a catchy pop tune. Saxophone and synths and electric guitars blasted from the speakers, and a group of girls at the front danced and sang along with the lead singer's cheery vocals. I stood on the steps that led to the backstage door and scanned the mob of faces. I couldn't see Nick anywhere. I searched the other room too, dodging barmen carrying stacks of glasses and pushing past couples making out. There was no sign of him there either. I really hoped he hadn't left for the bus already. Would he have gone without saying goodbye? Maybe Nick had been looking for me and hadn't been able to find me. That thought filled me with panic. I couldn't let another week go by with that horrible tension between us. He hadn't even texted me to tell me how his gig went. I needed to talk to him; I needed to apologize. I needed everything to go back to normal.

I spotted Sophie at the merchandise stand and made my way over to her. Dillon was standing behind it, arranging T-shirts and CDs into neat piles. He was really taking the 'Look busy' thing seriously. Ellie was standing by the door, holding a clipboard. I was careful to avoid her in case she asked me to do something. I'd explain the situation to Dillon later – maybe he'd cover for me.

'Soph,' I said, tapping her on the shoulder. 'Have you seen Nick?'

'Think he went out to the smoking area with the others,' she said as she rooted around in her purse. 'I know I have a fiver in here somewhere,' she mumbled to Dillon as she sifted through receipts.

'Jacki, look at this,' said Dillon, holding up a CD. 'That first band recorded a cover of "Waiting for the Man" – I wonder if it's any good.'

'Oh, cool,' I said, distracted.

'Did you like them? I thought they were class.'

Dillon was looking at me, expecting an answer, but I was so preoccupied that I'd already forgotten the question.

'Sorry, guys,' I said. 'I'll talk to you later. I really need to find Nick.'

Dillon raised an eyebrow then turned round and put the

CD back down on the table. I couldn't tell what he was thinking. I didn't even know why I was trying to work that out. Sophie looked at me disapprovingly, but I ignored it. She didn't understand how I felt about Nick and how urgent it was that I found him. I had to talk to Nick; I had to fix things between us. I'd make it up to her later.

As I hurried up the stairs, Andrew was strutting down. He was checking out the girl in front of him so intently that he didn't even see me. I rolled my eyes. For a split second I considered asking him more about the picture, but I just couldn't bring myself to do it. This was too important. I'd call him tomorrow. I had to concentrate on my own problems first.

I finally made it to the smoking area and saw Nick near the back, talking to Chris and Fitz, our friends from Avarna. He was facing away from me, his head bowed as he laughed loudly. Chris nodded at me and Nick turned round. He suddenly looked serious. He walked towards me, and without actually touching me, led me towards the bench in the corner. I could tell he was annoyed, but I was sure that everything was going to be OK. I was going to apologize. He sat down and I sat right beside him. I tried to hold his hand, but he brushed me away.

'I'm sorry,' I said. 'I know I didn't spend much time with you tonight. I was just so busy. We had all these tasks to do for the magazine and then I had to perform as well.' He looked unimpressed. He obviously didn't want to hear about that. 'I know things haven't been great between us,' I carried on, 'but that's because we haven't been spending much time together. I'll be home in Avarna soon and things will go back to the way they used to be.'

'Will they though?' said Nick, without looking at me. He was pulling at a loose thread on his denims, like he always did when he was trying to think of what to say.

'Of course,' I said. And I really meant it. I knew we'd gone through a rough patch, but I was sure that was over now.

'I don't know, Jacki,' he said with a sigh. 'I try so hard to make you happy, but it's never good enough.'

'What do you mean?' I asked, confused. I wondered why he was talking like this. He didn't sound himself; his voice seemed different, rehearsed. It was like I was listening to somebody else.

'Being with you . . .' he said. 'It's just so exhausting. I feel like you're watching everything I do . . . waiting for me to mess up.'

There was no warmth in his words. It was like he was talking to a stranger. The word 'exhausting' echoed in my head. I was trying to make things right, why was he being like this?

'I just find you so draining.'

'Oh, I'm sorry,' I said, feeling anger rising inside me. 'It must take a lot out of you to have to send one text message every *four* days.'

He didn't seem to have a comeback for this, so I kept talking.

'No, I'm serious,' I said. 'Poor you! You should probably go on a holiday or something. Try to recover from how *exhausting* I am.'

'Will you just drop the texting thing?' he said. 'I told you I had a lot going on this week.'

'Yeah, I know. But what's the point of all this if you don't even want to talk to me? You must not like me very much any more!' I was practically shouting at him, and still he refused to look me directly in the eye, which was making me even angrier.

'I do like you though,' he said, finally looking at me. 'That's what's so frustrating about all of this! I *do* like you, but nothing is ever good enough!'

'Oh, come *on*, Nick, don't try to turn this round on me. If you had made even the slightest bit of effort, then we wouldn't be having this fight! What am I supposed to do? Ignore all the crappy stuff you do? Sit back and say nothing while you act like a total jerk? I'm not going to let you walk all over me. I tried keeping everything inside, I really tried! It didn't make things any better!'

This was so infuriating. I couldn't believe he was blaming me for this. I wasn't the one who'd changed. I wasn't the one who'd stopped caring.

'I don't see what the big deal is,' he said. 'So I didn't text you – wow, what a crime.' And he had that indignant look on his face. I wasn't going to censor my words any more. He was being so cruel, I wasn't going to hold back either.

'I think you were punishing me,' I said. 'For not going to your gig.'

'Well then, you're crazy. I didn't text you because I just didn't feel like it. I knew I'd be seeing you today. I was going to tell you then. Can you just drop it?'

'And the fact that you never want to call me means that we have a problem,' I said, moving down the bench, away from him. I couldn't believe he was acting like this.

'Why didn't you call *me*, huh?' he said. 'Why didn't you ask *me* how *my* gig went?'

'Why should I?' I was actually shouting now. 'I'm always the one making the effort!'

He just shrugged.

'Why can't you just say sorry?' I said desperately. 'Why can't you just admit that you were wrong? Would that really be so hard?'

'I'm not saying sorry. Because I didn't do anything!'

I was aware that most of the people in the smoking area were now watching us, but I didn't even care. I was so angry I was about to cry. I pressed the tips of my fingers against my eyes, as if hoping to force the tears back in. Neither of us said anything for a while, until Nick finally spoke.

'I think we should break up,' he said.

'*What?*'

'I don't think we're right for each other any more. I don't think we should keep going on like this.'

'You don't mean that,' I said, lifting my head. But when I saw the look on his face I started to panic. There was no anger there. He just looked like he wasn't bothered any more. He was serious. I felt like everything was collapsing around me. I felt like nothing else mattered apart from what was happening right now on this bench. I told myself he meant everything to me. I needed to fix this, but I didn't know what to say. I didn't know how to reverse the damage I'd done.

'I can't do this any more,' he said. 'I don't think we're right for each other.'

'We are,' I said, fighting back tears. I couldn't bear this. We were meant to have made up by now. This wasn't supposed to happen.

'I didn't mean it,' I said. 'I was just angry. I'm under a lot of pressure. I didn't mean to say those things. I didn't mean that we should actually break up. Stop for a second and think about what you're saying. Think about what you're throwing away.'

'I'm sorry, Jacki,' he said. 'This is how it has to be. I've been thinking about it for a while. I don't think we should force this any more.'

The indifference in his voice upset me so much. He didn't seem upset at all; it was like he didn't care what this was doing to me. He didn't care that I could hardly breathe, that I was about to burst into tears. Why was he doing this to me now? He knew how much stress I was under. I couldn't hold it back any longer. I started to cry. He just sat there, watching me. Chris and Fitz walked in our direction and then hovered awkwardly near the bench. They seemed to be as shocked about this as I was. Chris looked at me sympathetically, but Fitz just glared at Nick as if to say hurry up.

'I have to get the bus,' said Nick. 'Will you be all right?'

Was he for real? Did he actually just say that?

'Oh yes, I'll be fantastic,' I said, then buried my face in my hands.

'I'm sorry, Jacki,' he muttered.

I didn't say anything. I didn't look up. When I eventually did, they were gone. I rooted around in my bag for my phone. My hand was shaking as I scrolled down through the numbers, heavy tears dripping on to the screen.

'Hey,' said Hannah, picking up. 'Sorry I bailed – had to catch the bus. I have rehearsals at half eight.'

'He broke up with me,' I sobbed down the phone.

'What? Where are you?'

'The smoking area.' I wiped my eyes.

'I'll be there in ten minutes.'

'No, it's OK. I thought you were still here. Go home, I'll be fine.'

'Stay there,' she said. 'I'm getting off.'

'Seriously, it's –'

'Stop the bus!' she screamed, and then hung up.

'I mean, who the hell does he think he is?' said Hannah.

'What a total dickhead,' said Sophie. 'I'm so angry with him. SO angry with him . . . I hate him.'

'He's not even that hot,' said Hannah. 'He has a really big forehead.'

'That's true,' said Sophie. 'He does have a really big forehead.'

We sat in the ice-cream parlour across from Rage. It was empty apart from us and the ice-cream guy, who was drawing in his sketchbook and not taking any notice of our ranting. My mint choc-chip was melting into gloop and I swished it round with my spoon, unable to stomach it. Hannah and Sophie had been bitching about Nick for the past ten minutes, which did actually help to ease the pain a little. I wasn't taking part any more; I was writing him an extremely long text instead, trying to explain why I'd been so difficult.

'And he used the word literally in totally the wrong context once,' said Sophie.

'Yeah, that's a real deal-breaker,' said Hannah with a laugh.

'What? I'm trying to be helpful!' said Sophie.

'You're not texting Nick, are you?' asked Hannah, breaking off from their we-hate-Nick session and finally noticing what I was up to. I didn't even bother trying to lie. Hannah was an actress – she could spot even the most skilled of fakers.

'Jacki, give me your phone,' she said sternly.

'But a lot of it is my fault,' I said. 'I threatened him. I gave out to him for not sharing stuff with me. I said if he couldn't do that then what was the point of us?'

'Listen,' said Hannah. 'It's not your fault, OK? Something was obviously not right. You said so yourself last week.'

'I know . . . but I never really thought we'd actually break up. I just need to –'

'You should wait,' said Sophie. 'Wait until you've calmed down a bit, looked at things rationally, before you text him.'

'Whatever you say now is going to sound a little crazy,' said Hannah, 'no matter how good your intentions. I know you feel like the only thing you want to do right now is fix it, but you have to let him go. He chose to break up with you. He's a moron for doing it, and either you two weren't meant for each other, or he'll realize what a complete idiot he was and come running back. But he's going to have to realize that for himself. You couldn't control what happened tonight, but you can control what you do now. *Don't call him.*'

It was the only thing I wanted to do right now, but I could see Hannah's point. I deleted the half-written text without sending it and handed her my phone.

'You'll thank me later,' she said.

'They should really teach night classes on the subject of boys,' said Sophie, folding her napkin into the shape of a ship. 'Forget metaphysics, relationships are the real predicament.'

'Life is one big long relationship night class,' I said with a sigh.

Sophie smiled. 'A friend-ship,' she said, handing me the folded napkin. I giggled. I was so lucky to have such nice friends. Friends who convinced bus drivers to brake at undesignated stops and bought ice cream to cheer me up and lied about the level of my ex-boyfriend's hotness. I did wish Colin could be here too, even if he would just say I told you so. He'd been right about Nick. He'd said I was going to get hurt, and now I was hurting a lot. But even though Nick had hurt me so much, I was still sure I loved him. And I really wanted to talk to him. I wouldn't though. Not yet . . . I'd take Hannah's advice.

'Are you sure you're going to be OK?' said Sophie as we arrived at my gran's gate.

'Yes, I'll be fine,' I said.

Hannah handed me back my phone. 'Call me if you need anything,' she said.

'I will.'

'And don't call him,' she added.

'I won't.'

They forced me into a bear hug, only letting go when I'd been suitably squashed.

'Bye,' they said in unison.

'Bye,' I said, then pushed open the gate.

I opened the front door, stepped into the hallway, then closed the door as gently as possible behind me. It was so quiet, all the lights were off and Gran had gone to bed. In the silence the sadness suddenly hit me like a blow to the chest. I climbed the stairs, went into my bedroom, lay down on my bed and called Nick's number. It rang out. He didn't want to talk to me, he didn't want to see me, he didn't want to be with me. I felt so empty. I threw my phone on the floor, curled up into the smallest ball my body would allow and cried myself to sleep.

Chapter 18

There's something comforting in being alone. When you're alone, you can't get hurt. And yet we just keep going back for more, keep setting ourselves up for more pain. Because the hope for something great overrides the fear of getting rejected. And I think that's a wonderful thing, that we're willing to risk heartbreak because there is a very slight chance that this person might be the right person, that this person might actually love you forever. But I also think it sucks because at that moment I felt so, so horrible.

I couldn't get angry, and that's what I needed to be. I needed to get angry in order to get over Nick. When I could see him for what he really was, then I would be able to get over him. I was angry at myself for not being honest with him. Part of me knew he was moody and selfish and didn't deserve me, but just then all I wanted was for him to hold me. He'd told me he didn't want to be with me, that he didn't want to talk to me, but the only thing I wanted in the world right then was for him to put his arms round me. I knew it was completely illogical and I knew I shouldn't want it, but I did.

I lied to Gran and told her I had a migraine so that I

wouldn't have to go into work at the magazine. I just wanted to lock myself away, but at the same time it was torture to be alone. I wanted to talk to somebody, to get out some of what was in my head before I drove myself insane, analysing it over and over again, wondering how things would have gone if I hadn't been so stubborn and called him. But then the next second I was thinking, *No, why should I have to do everything? Why should I give in to his sulky moods and act like everything's great when it's clearly not?* Part of me hated Nick for doing this to me. Could he not have waited a few more days? He didn't know I was working on a case, but he did know I was working at *Electric* magazine. I wondered how long I could get away with calling in sick.

I heard my door creak. I pulled myself up, thinking it would be Gran offering me more tea. I couldn't stomach anything at the moment, not even tea, so I really didn't want any. To my surprise, I saw Hannah standing there.

'Jacki King,' she said, barging into my room. I'd just dumped all my stuff inside my door last night, so she had to climb over everything to get in.

'Yes?' I said.

'Get out of that bed.'

'I'm never getting out of this bed,' I said.

'So you're going to stay there forever?'

'Yes. I've decided I'm going to die of a broken heart.'

'You can't die of a broken heart, it's not possible.'

'Johnny Cash did.'

'He was seventy-one!'

'So?'

'And he and June were *meant* to be together.'

I ignored the last comment. Hannah was just being mean now.

'When was the last time you ate?'

'Can't remember.'

'How come you didn't go to work today?'

'How did you know I didn't go to the magazine?'

'Dillon told me. He was worried about you.'

'I'll be fine,' I said, trying not to think about the fact that Dillon had said he was worried about me. 'If I lie perfectly still and try not to move and try not to think, then I'm fine.'

'Have you heard from *him*?'

'No.'

'Are you going to the magazine tomorrow?'

'No.'

'Jacki, are you honestly going to let this take over your entire life? You need to get up.'

Hannah pulled the covers off my bed. I was wearing fleece pyjamas, bed socks and clutching a hot-water bottle.

'I'm cold,' I said. I actually did still feel sick and cold from yesterday. Having someone break up with you was obviously as physically painful as it was emotional.

'That's because you haven't moved in fifteen hours. Get up, we're going shopping! Sophie needs a new lens for her telescope and I need a new bra.'

'I don't want to go shopping.'

'You don't have a choice.'

'Aren't you meant to be in school?'

'It's sports day,' said Hannah. 'Sophie and I do not do sports day. Come on, we'll pick her up on the way there.'

Hannah opened the wardrobe and pulled out my denims and Janis Joplin T-shirt.

'Put these on,' she said.

Usually I love shopping. I adore looking at clothes and bags and shoes. I could do it for hours and not get bored. But today every step was a chore. I didn't want to be outside, I wanted to go back to bed. It took all of my energy to simply not start crying in public. Every song they play in shopping centres is a love song. Every. Single. One. Hundreds of songs filled with lies and empty promises and fake feelings. If they played Michael Bublé again I was going to crack. Hannah and Sophie tried their best to cheer me up, and I really did try not to be so grumpy, for their sake.

'What do you think?' asked Sophie, holding up a purple dress.

'I dunno,' said Hannah. 'It's not really you.'

'I like it,' I said. 'I bet it would look nice on.'

'I'll try it on,' said Sophie. 'If that's OK?'

'Yeah, sure,' I said.

I followed Hannah and Sophie around Dundrum shopping centre, but I wasn't really paying attention. Instead I was still analysing, still trying to figure out what Nick was thinking, but I couldn't. I think that's one of the major tragedies of life. It was funny how Kayla and Beth had been able to get inside my head, infiltrate my dreams, show me what had happened to them, and yet I didn't know what my own living boyfriend . . . living ex-boyfriend . . . was thinking. You can never get inside somebody else's head – you'll never be able to find out what they are really thinking. Even when someone tells you, you don't really know. And I think that's what hurt the most. Not the rejection or the betrayal. It was the not knowing what was going through his head in that split second when he decided that what we had just wasn't worth holding on to. That moment when he decided I was disposable.

I could hear Colin's words ringing in my ears – 'You need to cut that loose, Jacki, because he's not treating you right.'

Hannah held up two different eye shadows.

'Which one?' she said.

I shrugged.

'You should buy a dress,' she said. 'That'll make you feel better. And you need something to wear to karaoke at Rage on Friday.'

'Oh, I dunno, Han, I don't think I'm up for karaoke.'

'But you LOVE karaoke,' she said.

I somehow managed to make it through to lunch and we sat up on the stools at the sushi counter. I watched the brightly coloured plastic cartons go by on the conveyor belt. Hannah and Sophie were discussing their purchases. After much persuasion from Hannah I'd bought something. Usually I'd be excited about finding such a nice dress in exactly the right size, but nothing could cheer me up today. I still wasn't hungry either. I wasn't even going to attempt to eat. If Hannah and Sophie were getting tired of my mood, they didn't say anything. I guess you get a free pass when something like this happens. Because everyone knows what it's like to be dumped. And if they don't they're lucky.

When I got home, I promised Hannah I wouldn't get back

into bed, so instead I decided to write some lyrics. It wasn't very enjoyable though because I just ended up writing particularly angry stuff.

> *A disposable camera*
> *In the back of your drawer;*
> *Distant memories*
> *That's what I'm good for.*
>
> *Something fun*
> *But you'd rather forget;*
> *Listen up, baby,*
> *I'm not quite done yet.*
>
> *Were you getting bored*
> *With my modest demands?*
> *I'm sorry I don't like*
> *Your favourite bands.*
>
> *Might want to consider*
> *Before you throw me away;*
> *Chances are you'll*
> *Be back some day.*
>
> *Eighteen red roses*
> *Waiting by my door*
> *But distant memories*
> *That's what you're good for.*

Chapter 19

The next morning I was at *Electric* magazine, feeling only slightly better. On top of everything that had happened with Nick, I was obviously coming down with something. This only added to my grumpiness. I tried to keep busy, but there wasn't much to do. I think Ellie thought my bad mood was somehow related to the case, that I was worn out from working so hard on it, so she hadn't given me much work. This made me feel guilty on top of everything else. I felt like I'd abandoned Kayla over the last few days. I'd been so obsessed with my own problems that I'd forgotten the real reason I was in Dublin. I had to snap out of it.

'Are you OK?' said Dillon, taking off his headphones.

'Yeah,' I lied. 'I'm just really tired.'

I'd decided not to tell him about Nick, mainly because whenever I attempted to tell anyone my eyes welled up with tears. I was sure he'd find out eventually anyway.

'I can't believe the two weeks are almost up,' he said, looking at me intently. 'I wish I could stay here forever. I'll miss doing all this with you, Jacki.'

I stopped in my tracks. Did he just say he was going to miss me? No, no. He just meant he'd miss *working* with me.

I peeped up at him, trying to form a sensible response, but was too flustered by the way he was looking at me and by everything that had happened with Nick.

'Um, yeah. I'll miss it too.' I stumbled over my words. 'I –'

'Jacki, Dillon, will you come into the office for a moment?' Ellie called us in and with the tension of the moment suddenly broken, I wasn't sure if I felt relieved or not.

We were ushered in and Ellie shut the door. 'I'll show you some photos of the location for tomorrow's shoot,' she said. 'It's just perfect; it's so bleak, it really captures the mood of the –'

'Oh my god!' I blurted as she enlarged the picture.

Ellie turned round and looked at me, surprised.

'It's . . . it's just so beautiful!' I said.

'Isn't it just! I'm glad you think so too. So, hair and make-up starts at seven a.m. . . .'

As Ellie filled us in with the rest of the details of the shoot, I stood at the desk staring at the photo in a daze. It was like somebody had taken a snapshot of my dream and put it on the Internet. I know lots of roads look the same, but this was unbelievably similar. I felt a shiver run down my back. I could hear the clinking of the camera and the clip-clop of the heels and I could see the brown eyes of the man in the balaclava.

'Jacki,' said Ellie. 'You don't look well at all. Do you want to go home?'

'No thanks,' I said. 'I'll be fine.'

I would. I had to be. This was clearly a sign.

One thing I learned the next morning was that it's really, REALLY cold in the Dublin mountains at 7 a.m., even in

May. Ellie, Cliona and Patricia were all wearing fur jackets – they'd obviously done this before. I tried to stop shivering and concentrate on what I had to do. Willis Middleton was sitting on one of those director's chairs, wearing skinny jeans, a loose white T-shirt, a black leather jacket and lots of beads round his neck. He was holding a copy of his latest record, a concept album entitled *Fear*.

'And for one last question . . . what scares you?' asked the reporter, in a very serious voice.

'Hmm . . . I'm not sure,' said Willis. 'I guess . . . nothing!'

Willis rarely does interviews, so everybody had been warned to be extra nice to him. 'Humour him,' were the words Ellie had used. I was too busy looking around, hoping to see the barbed-wire fence. We'd driven up a road that was uncannily similar to the one from my dream and walked through the unkempt grass, but I was yet to find the most important place. I thought maybe I'd see Kayla, but nothing had happened yet. I tried wandering off a few times, but each time Ellie would call me back to make sure Willis had enough water or enough choc-chip cookies. He actually wasn't that demanding at all. I think he'd calmed down a lot since coming out of rehab. He'd been telling me how he didn't drink coffee any more when I'd offered him some because he found it interfered with his meditation. He didn't seem that crazy at all. But the *Electric* staff were all still pretty on edge, like he was a ticking time bomb that could go off at any second. I myself felt really sick, and wondered if it was from lack of sleep.

When it was time for Willis to get his photographs taken, Dillon and I walked him back to his trailer, and he changed into what looked like the exact same pair of skinny jeans.

'Stay right there, that's perfect,' said the photographer. 'These are great.' I was getting frustrated. Surely this would be over soon? How many photos of Willis with his legs crossed, leaning slightly forward in the middle of the road, did they actually need? After what felt like an age, they moved him over to the trees, and then further into the field to get some more shots. Ellie asked Dillon and me to stay behind and start packing up all the outfits, none of which Willis had actually agreed to wear. I didn't blame him – some of them looked seriously dodgy.

'That's a wrap, folks,' said Ellie a few minutes later.

'Brilliant,' said Willis. 'This means I'll be able to catch my flight to New York after all.'

Ellie smiled, obviously delighted that the whole thing had gone off without a hitch. But her expression soon changed when she saw the anxious look on Willis's face.

'Crap,' he said. 'I think I must have dropped my Zippo . . . my wife got it for me for our anniversary – it's engraved and everything. She's going to KILL me.'

'Jacki will find it,' said Ellie with such assurance that it actually scared me. I already felt sick and I was in no state to be left in charge of finding an expensive and sentimental lighter. I trudged into the field, muck clinging to my Converse. I walked in the same direction they'd taken, hoping to see a glint of silver in among all the grass, but I found nothing. I kept looking and looking and I could hear Ellie calling my name, but I didn't answer. What did she think I was, some sort of miracle worker? Then I saw it; not the lighter, but the barbed-wire fence.

It ran between the field we were in and the next. I rushed

over to it and got the strangest feeling. I felt like I was sinking, even though I was standing perfectly still. I felt like everything was moving around me, just like I had the first time I'd dreamed about Kayla. Then I saw her, out of the corner of my eye, her red hair speeding past me in a blur.

This was it. I'd found it – I'd found her grave. I couldn't believe it. I had to tell Detective Sergeant Lawlor straight away.

Then, on the other side of the fence I saw something glinting in the sunlight – Willis's lighter. I made a mental note of exactly where I was, then took a few pictures on my phone, just to be sure I could find the place again. Then I rushed back to the others.

'Oh, wow,' said Willis. 'Thank you so much! You're an angel.'

'It's OK, no big deal,' I said.

'No, you don't understand – the missus would actually have murdered me. I don't usually do this,' he said, 'but here's my card.' He handed me his business card and smiled. Then he said goodbye to everyone and got into his car. He gave me the call-me signal from the window.

'If you're ever in NY, hit me up,' he shouted as the car pulled away.

'Wow. Well done, Jacki!' said Dillon, putting his hand on my arm. We both realized what he had done and stepped apart hastily.

'Dillon, I . . . er . . . I need to make a call.'

And I stumbled off.

Matt answered straight away.

'I think I know where she's buried,' I said.

'You serious?'

'Yes. I've got an exact location – it's in the Dublin mountains. There's obviously no sign of a grave now because it's all overgrown, but I know she's buried there, I'd bet my life on it. We have to start digging.'

'It doesn't work like that, Jacki. I can't just start digging. I need to give the team a reason.'

'I'm giving you one. I have a strong feeling that she's buried down there.'

'I need a name, Jacki. I need some evidence. Detective Sergeant Lonergan is concerned that you haven't come up with a name for us yet. Now this isn't my view at all. I'm just telling you what he said. I told him that you are the best there is and that you'll have something for us when the time is right, but he's getting impatient.'

'What exactly did he say?' I asked. 'Tell me, I can handle it.'

'He said . . . he said he doesn't know if you're up to it.'

'I know where she's buried.'

'I need a warrant to search there, and I can't get one of those without –'

'Fine,' I said. 'I'm still working on it. I'll do everything I can to get you a name. Just hold on for another little while.'

Now that I'd found where I believed she was buried, I suddenly had a renewed passion for solving the case. I'd let the real reason I was in Dublin get all swallowed up by everything that was happening in my love life (or lack of) and I felt bad. I was going to give Kayla justice and solve this case once and for all.

I called Andrew and asked to meet him at the ice-cream place. He started to protest, muttering something about going to Calum's, but eventually agreed.

When I got there, Andrew was sitting by himself in a corner of the café, tapping his fingers on the table. It was really obvious he didn't want to be there. He nodded when he saw me, but didn't smile. That was fine with me – I didn't need a welcoming committee. I just had one question I needed him to answer.

'Would you like to explain this?' I said, showing him the photograph of Kayla in the jersey.

'I didn't take that,' he said.

'It was on your phone.'

'So? It's on a few people's phones.'

'What?'

'Calum sent it to us when none of us would believe he'd slept with Kayla. That's her, and she's wearing his jersey. I honestly thought he was making it up, but that's definitely his. And I doubt he would have gone to the trouble of stealing that picture from her.'

I hated to admit it, but I had a feeling he was telling the truth. I could ask the others, but I pretty much knew they would corroborate what Andrew said.

I was back at square one and still no closer to helping the girl who haunted my dreams.

Chapter 20

Whenever we're in the same city, Hannah and I always get ready to go out together. It's like a ritual. I go over to her house, or she comes over to mine, and we gossip as we listen to music and apply eye shadow and try to decide which top to wear. Right now I was at hers, watching as she stood on her bed, singing along to the Rolling Stones. I was wearing my new black dress, even though I felt like putting on my pyjamas and going back to bed. I still wasn't feeling great – in fact I felt terrible. But I had to admit there was a possibility that Hannah was right – that forcing myself to go out and be sociable might actually make things better. So I was going to try it. I still hadn't heard from Nick. I wasn't proud of it, but I'd sent him one last text, asking him to talk to me. I'd regretted it immediately. I knew deep down that he probably wasn't going to answer. I hadn't told Hannah. I couldn't deal with the disapproving glances that would follow that sort of confession.

'So, who's coming out tonight?' I asked.

'Ross,' said Hannah. 'And Sophie says she hates karaoke, but I reckon we'll get around her. That's it, I think, just the four of us. Not that many people were up for it.'

'Yeah, how come your mum's letting you go?' I said. She was usually pretty strict, not that it ever actually stopped Hannah.

'I told her you were broken-hearted and needed a distraction.'

'Stop using my situation to feed your karaoke habit.'

Hazel had told me I could bring some friends to karaoke night in Rage for free. It was so nice of her. She hardly even knew me.

'I dunno what I should sing,' said Hannah. 'Should I go for a classic or sing something a bit more out there?' Hannah took karaoke way too seriously. She'd been attending musical theatre classes since she was four and had a very good voice. Although it wasn't her first love, she wanted to be one of those actors who could also sing well if required.

'Oh, I asked Dillon if he wanted to come,' I said. I had kind of done it without thinking. He'd asked me what I was doing that evening and I'd invited him along. I told him he should definitely try to make it. Initially I'd been kind of embarrassed – it sounded like I really wanted him to go – but then I thought, *Why not?* It's not like anything was going to happen and I didn't have Nick around any more to get jealous about it.

'Dillon?' said Hannah.

'Yeah, well, we did work together. He said he's going to check with his friends and he might drop along later. I dunno if he will . . . he might.'

'Oh my god,' said Hannah.

'What?'

'You like him.'

'What? No I don't.'

'You DO! You like Dillon!'

'We're just friends.'

'You like Dillon. You're right though. He is cute, especially since he cut his hair.'

'I didn't say he was cute, Hannah.'

'How long have you liked him for? Why didn't I spot this before? I suppose I wasn't looking out for it. But now that you've got rid of that other tool . . . Are you going to kiss him? Or is it too soon?'

'Hannah, I don't even know if he likes me. I don't know if I like him!'

'Aha! You *do* like him!'

'I didn't say that!' My cheeks turned red.

'I knew it! Aww! That's so cute. Dillon and Jacki, Jacki and Dillon. Jacki –'

I picked up the cushion from her desk chair and threw it at her.

'OK!' she said. 'I'll stop. He is cute though.'

'Yeah,' I said, admitting it to myself for the very first time. 'He is.'

Rage had become one of my new favourite places. I just loved everything about it. I was happy to be there now; we'd even managed to drag Sophie along. Karaoke was due to begin in a few minutes and I was starting to feel a bit better. We were sitting at a table near the stage and already the place was packed. Hannah flicked through the list of songs. I knew this was exactly the kind of thing that Colin would love. I wished he was here, and I was tempted to text him, but I couldn't face the thought of another person ignoring me. I just didn't think I'd be able to handle it. I'd been so horrible to him after Nick had left me at the theatre that night, I wasn't sure what to say to make it better.

'What are you going to sing?' Hannah asked me. 'I'm torn between a few.'

'I dunno,' I said. 'There are so many classics.'

'It's all right for you guys,' said Sophie. 'You're the only ones who can sing.'

'Er, speak for yourself,' said Ross. Ross liked singing, but he hadn't got a note in his head.

'Ah, come on, Soph, it's only a bit of fun,' said Hannah. 'You have to sing something.'

Sophie reluctantly took the song list off her.

I looked up and saw Dillon coming through the doorway. I watched him as he walked through the crowd. He was wearing his blue check shirt, the same one he'd worn on our first day in *Electric*.

'Hey, guys,' he said when he'd arrived at our table. 'Mark and the others couldn't make it.' He sat down on the stool beside me. 'God, I hate karaoke,' he added.

'Finally,' said Sophie, 'somebody who agrees with me!'

'How come you're here then?' I asked, laughing.

'Um . . . because you said you would be.'

I blushed. I didn't think any of the others had heard him. I tried to come up with something clever to say back, to distract me from how I was feeling, but the words wouldn't come and I ended up looking at the floor. Not a very smooth move, but I wasn't quite ready to suggest to Dillon that I had feelings for him. It would mean a final closure on everything I'd had with Nick. And as much as I hated him for what he'd done to me and really wanted to let go, I wasn't able to do that just yet.

Hannah kicked me under the table, then winked. Oh good. Someone *had* heard what Dillon said.

I kicked her back and tried to look angry, but even though I was confused, I couldn't help smiling.

'We need some really bad singing,' said Dillon, who had noticed Hannah's antics. He picked up the song list. I realized he had deliberately moved things on to make me feel less awkward. He went up and added his name to the list.

About fifteen minutes later, he was nervously approaching the mic. The intro to Thin Lizzy's 'Old Town' came on, and I cheered. 'This one's for Jacki,' he said. His voice was actually not bad, and when he smiled at me I couldn't help but feel so much better.

'I'm just going out to get some air,' I said to Hannah several songs later. The weird sickness I'd been feeling all week had come over me again and I needed some space.

I stepped into Rage's outside terraced area, its ceiling covered in hundreds of tiny twinkling fairy lights, and was surprised to see Dillon already leaning against the balcony.

'Hi, Jacki,' he said. 'Are you not gonna sing? I suppose I can't blame you. It'd be hard to beat my performance.'

I laughed despite how I felt. 'You'd think. I'm actually not feeling that great so I came out for the air.'

'Well, I'm glad you're here anyway.'

I shivered in the cold. Dillon saw and moved towards me, taking off his coat. 'Here, put this on.'

'No, it's OK. I . . .' Dillon's hand brushed against my neck as he pulled his coat tightly round me. The touch sent my heart beating faster. He moved slowly closer to me. I didn't move away. Then he leaned forward and kissed me. His lips met mine and for a moment it felt amazing – breathtaking and electric. But, just as quickly as it had happened, I realized what I was doing and pulled back.

'What's wrong. Are you OK?' Dillon asked, looking worried. 'I'm sorry, I just . . . I thought you wanted to –'

'No, it's not you, I promise.' I shook my head sadly. 'Listen, Dillon, I like you, I really do. But I don't think I can do anything about it at the moment. This is going to sound like an excuse, but I swear it's not. I just have to be honest – I'm not entirely over Nick. I like you, but I don't think I can get into anything right now. I don't think it would be fair to you, I'm just such a mess. I know I shouldn't be with Nick, and I hate him so much, but I can't let go of all the feelings I have for him. I wish they would just disappear.'

I didn't want anything I had with Dillon to be tainted by this sadness. I was still waiting for my heart to catch up with my head.

'Do you . . . do you ever think you'll be over him?' he asked.

'Yeah, of course, I mean . . . I know I will. Sophie has this theory. She reckons you count up the number of days you went out with a person, and then divide it by three, and that's the amount of time it'll take you to get over them.'

'How long were you going out with Nick for?' he asked.

'Um . . . two hundred and fifty-two days,' I said, doing the calculations quickly in my head.

'Right. I'm going to look you up in eighty-four days so,' he said with a laugh.

I couldn't tell if he was serious. He kissed me on the cheek. 'Goodbye, Jacki,' he said. And I felt my heart crumble just a little.

Chapter 21

I wandered back into the club alone. I seemed to be making a habit of it these days. Hannah was on stage belting out 'I Love Rock 'n' Roll' at the top of her voice, complete with Britney-inspired dance moves that got more than one wolf-whistle from the crowd. I smiled and cheered her on as best I could, but the sick feeling had returned and I was starting to feel quite dizzy.

I looked up at Hannah, body-rolling against the mic, and willed myself to feel better. I didn't have time for this. Ten days had already passed by and I still had nothing real to show Matt – no hard evidence that would put an end to Kayla's case. Although I was certain I knew where her body was, I still didn't have a name to give him. There were people I didn't trust – Calum and Andrew especially – but I was wary of jumping to conclusions. I decided I should talk to them both again, try to figure out if they were hiding something.

I wanted to forget about what Matt Lawlor's detective sergeant had said about me, but I couldn't seem to let it go. Maybe a tiny part of me agreed with him. Just because I'd solved one murder didn't automatically mean I'd be able to solve another. Matt had so much faith in me, I didn't want to let him down. And I wanted to prove Detective Sergeant Lonergan wrong. I'd tried to earn his respect, but the only way I was going to do that was by getting results. He was right: I didn't have anything to show yet. But I'd stood in the place where Kayla was buried and I was going to get justice for her. No matter how long it took.

I knew that communicating with spirits could be draining, but I was doing what Ger had said – I was imagining a white light around me, protecting me. And I was wearing the bracelet, even though I wanted to rip it off my arm every time I saw it. I was shielding myself in every possible way, yet I still felt awful. My vision was blurry and I tried to focus, but big black patches appeared in front of my eyes. I blinked in the hope that they would go away, but they just got bigger, and soon I could see hardly anything but blackness. I took a deep breath and visualized the white light again, so bright that it hurt to look at it.

Eventually my sight went back to normal. I was still nauseous though, and my whole body was sore. I can safely say I'd never felt this bad before. Even last summer, I hadn't felt this weak.

Hannah sang the last line and I painfully forced myself to clap along with everyone else, then stood up and made my way over to the bar. I needed a drink of water. I could hardly walk straight and kept accidentally bumping into people. I could hear them sighing and tutting as I stumbled away. Maybe the white light wasn't working because I was exhausted. I hadn't got much sleep this week and my emotions were all over the place. I thought maybe it was more than that though. I had so little energy left – I could barely function. This wasn't heartbreak or fatigue, this was something else. Kayla was probably trying to give me a sign; maybe she was even here. I'd have to figure out what she was trying to tell me, but first I'd have to concentrate on not collapsing.

I tried to catch the barman's attention. Some guy was giving an impassioned, but tuneless rendition of a Bon Jovi song now, and the crowd had started to talk again.

'Are you OK?' asked a girl standing next to me.

'Yeah,' I said self-consciously. 'Why?'

She didn't answer, just glanced away awkwardly. I must have looked really bad. I abandoned the bar and headed for the bathroom. I hurried through the crowd and pushed open the door. There was a queue, but I managed to squeeze up to the sinks. I looked in the mirror and almost didn't recognize myself. My skin was so pale, my lips were practically blue and my eyes were all bloodshot. This was definitely not normal. I could see a group of girls in the reflection, whispering and staring at me. I rushed into a cubicle and locked the door. I felt so faint, I was afraid I was going to collapse. I no longer thought it was Kayla giving me a sign – she surely wouldn't do this to me. I was way too sick. Had someone spiked my drink? I didn't think so as I had got my own.

Ger's words flashed through my mind, 'Don't trust everybody you meet through this kind of work,' and it began to dawn on me that maybe I was being psychically attacked. I concentrated hard on doing everything Ger had told me to protect myself, but ten minutes passed and I still didn't feel any better. I was getting weaker and weaker by the second. I was too tired to even move, so I took out my phone to call somebody. Then I realized that I didn't have anybody to call. If I told Hannah or Sophie or even Matt, they'd all tell me to go to the hospital. I couldn't blame them – that was the normal reaction to something like this. I started to panic, but I tried not to cry. I had to calm down. I wondered who was doing this to me. I was so angry, but I didn't have a clue who was behind it.

I decided I was going to try and leave the bathroom, but I could hardly stand up. The graffiti on the cubicle walls danced before my eyes, the letters all moving in different directions, words joining up to make no sense. I dropped the lid of the toilet seat and sat down with my head in my hands. Then I started to drift off.

My head snapped back with a jolt. I'd fainted, but I didn't know how long I'd been out for. There was a knock on the door. I ignored it.

'Pee faster!' shrieked a girl on the other side.

I didn't know what to do. I thought I should probably just give in and ask for help, but there was nobody here who would understand. Hot tears started to well up in my eyes. I felt so powerless. And then it occurred to me – there was somebody who might be able to help: Lauren. She was a fortune-teller – maybe she'd heard about psychic attacks. She might know how to stop this, or at the very least she wouldn't think I was crazy. I sent her a text asking her to come to Rage if she was nearby, that it was an emergency. Then I took a deep breath and headed back out to the bar. She replied immediately. **I'm on my way**, she said.

I waited by the door instead of going over to our table. I didn't want the others to see me like this.

About fifteen minutes later Lauren rushed in. She looked like she'd been on a night out – she was wearing a black dress with a lace collar and red peep-toe shoes. As soon as she spotted me, her face turned completely pale. I couldn't blame her – I looked terrible.

'Thanks for coming,' I said. 'I didn't know who else to call.'

'I thought you'd gone home,' she said. 'Hazel told me you went back to Leitrim . . .'

'No, I just took a few days off,' I said, leaning against the wall to steady myself.

'You don't look good.'

She scanned my body, seeming to understand that something was very wrong. I felt so much better now that she was here.

'I'm in trouble,' I said. 'I'm pretty sure I'm being psychically attacked. Do you know anything about this kind of stuff?'

'A bit,' she said, looking scared. I felt bad for dragging her into this, but I had nowhere else to turn.

'I don't understand it,' I said. 'I've been protecting myself. But look at me . . . I look awful.'

'Do you know who's doing this?' she asked.

'No,' I said, 'I haven't a clue.'

She grabbed my arm and started to push through the crowd.

'Lauren, where are we going?'

'It could be a Difodi Curse,' she said. 'We can't waste any time.' She led me into the dressing room and my heart started to pound so fast it was unbearable. I recognized that name – Ger had warned me about this.

I almost tripped over the leads on the floor, but managed to make my way through the mess. I sat down on an amp and tried to take deep breaths. Lauren locked the dressing-room door and then hurried over to me.

'They've cursed something,' she said. 'Take off all your jewellery.'

I fumbled with my guitar-string bracelet from Nick. My fingers trembled as I tried to open the clasp.

'Quickly!' she said. She sounded so frightened, it made me panic.

'I'm going to be OK, right?' I was hoping she knew a way round it, like a loophole or something.

'We need to find the object now,' she said, 'to get the curse removed.'

'But only the person who performed the curse can lift it, isn't that true?'

Lauren didn't answer. My mind was racing with questions. Were we going to figure it out in time? Would we be able to reason with the person who was trying to kill me?

'How much time do I have left?' I asked.

'I'm not sure, but you haven't reached the worst part yet,' she said. I handed her the bracelet. She clutched it and closed her eyes. 'No, that's not it,' she said. 'Give me your bag.'

I handed it to her and she emptied its entire contents out on to the table. My wallet and make-up and phone and iPod were all scattered everywhere. She picked them up one by one – first my pocket mirror. 'No,' she said, and dropped it to the floor. Then my keys. 'No.' She did the same with the rest of my stuff as I took off every piece of jewellery I was wearing.

'No . . . no . . . no . . . no.'

I handed her the bundle of bracelets and rings.

'No . . . no . . . no . . . no,' she said, as they each fell with a clink on the floor. 'Are you sure there's nothing else?'

'I don't think so.' I started to cough, covered my mouth with my hand and felt a stab of fear as I took it away. I'd coughed up blood.

'Jacki, think! We don't have much time. We need to find the object!'

'But only the person who performed the curse can break it!' I said. 'Is that true?'

She didn't answer.

'Is that true, Lauren?'

Why was I even asking? I knew very well that it was. I was going to die.

'We need to find it *now*.'

She was trying to ease the pain – that was nice of her – but whether I died slowly or in agony didn't really make much of a difference. I was still going to die.

'Listen to me,' she said, grabbing my shoulders. 'Are you wearing any more jewellery? You must be.'

That's when I felt it in my pocket, against my hip. My hand was shaking so much, but I managed to grab hold of Kayla's star-shaped necklace and pull it out.

'Yes, yes, that's it!'

She snatched it from me. She was going to destroy it. This was going to ease the pain, but I was so scared. There was so much I had left to do. I couldn't die without seeing

Nick – or Dillon – again. I couldn't die without apologizing to Colin. And I still had to see my little brother or sister. I had to solve this case and make a record and go to New York and do all the things I still wanted to do.

Lauren knelt down and started to mumble something in a different language. It sounded a bit like Irish. I wondered what she was doing.

I touched her shoulder, but she pushed me away. She continued to mumble, swaying back and forth in a trance-like state. I tried to figure out what was going on. And then it hit me. I couldn't believe it. I was so relieved and yet so furious at the same time. She started to talk more loudly, her words booming through the dressing room.

I was so angry. I wanted to hurt her like she'd hurt me. But I didn't dare touch her, at least not until she'd finished. She was shouting now, but I doubted anybody else could hear her. The music from outside was drowning her out.

After a few minutes she stopped swaying and sat perfectly still. I could smell burning. She opened her hands. The outline of a star had been scalded into each palm.

'Only the person who performed the curse can break it,' I said. 'Only –'

'Not always,' said Lauren, her voice trembling.

'I'm not stupid!' I said. 'It was you!'

She stood up. I was so mad that I pushed her against the wall.

'You almost killed me!' I yelled. 'I could have died! You knew what *object* we were looking for. Why didn't you just tell me to give you the necklace?'

'I didn't want you to know it was me. I'm sorry, Jacki, I'm so, so sorry.'

I should have suspected her sooner – I was aware of her supernatural ability.

'You killed Kayla . . .' I said. 'How did you do it? Did you curse her?'

'No,' said Lauren. 'No, I swear I didn't hurt Kayla. I don't know what happened to her. Somebody paid me to do this, to get rid of you. They didn't want you interfering.'

I grabbed the collar of her dress and pushed her further up the wall.

'Who?'

'I can't tell you.'

'Give me a name.'

'You know I can't. You know –'

'– that if you reveal the details of the curse you'll incur *torturous pain*? Yes, I know, I've read all about the Difodi Curse. But what do you think *I've* just been through?'

'Jacki, please.'

'Give me some information,' I said, 'or I swear to god I'll –'

'It's a couple,' she said. 'Or at least they were a couple, I'm not sure if they still are. They were both at the party. They approached me last week, paid me to do this.' She started to sob. I could smell burning and realized it was coming from her hands. The star-shaped scars were opening up.

'Keep going!' I shouted. 'What else do you know?'

'I owe them one. They gave me money when I needed it, years ago, and now they're guilting me into helping them.

If somebody with paranormal powers gets involved with Kayla's case, they ask me to deal with it. When that psychic came forward last year and offered to help they made me get rid of him. Not that he knew anything anyway. They told me you were young and it shouldn't take much to get rid of you. I psychically attacked that other guy too, just sent him some negative vibes, and he was gone in less than three days. When I heard you were only sixteen, I thought you'd be gone within a few days too, that it would all be fine. I never expected you to last this long. When I saw you the other day I was going to lift the curse there and then. I told them it had gone too far, that it was too dangerous. When I heard you'd gone home, I was so relieved. I thought it was over. I never meant to kill you – you have to believe me. I'm sorry. I'm so, so sorry.'

'Tell me who they are.'

'Please, Jacki,' she said, showing me her hands. 'Please don't make me tell you.'

She started to cry. I couldn't do it. I couldn't cause her that much pain, even though she'd almost killed me. I loosened my grip.

'Thank you,' she said. 'Thank you, thank you, thank you.'

'Don't thank me. You're only getting away with this because I don't have the guts to hurt you.'

'I'm sorry, Jacki, I'm so, so sorry.'

'I don't want your apology,' I said as I stormed out and slammed the door behind me.

Chapter 22

A couple. It must have been Amy and Andrew – unless there was something I had missed. Perhaps everyone had been right to be angry at them for Kayla's disappearance.

I stood outside Rage, considering my next move. Temple Bar was packed with people out for the night. There were lots of students celebrating the last days of term. Girls in high heels tottered around, unsteady on the cobblestones, and groups of guys strutted past, shouting and joking. I decided to ring Ellie. I figured she was the safest person to contact.

'Hi, Jacki,' she said. 'Is everything OK?'

'I'm sorry for calling so late,' I said. 'I hope I didn't wake you?'

'Nope, me and Sasha are just having a movie night. What's up?'

'I need your help with something.'

'Where are you?' she said. 'It's really loud, I can hardly hear you.'

'I'm outside Rage. Hold on, I'll move away from the door.' I wove though the crowds, away from the blaring music.

'Do you wanna come over?' she said. 'We're just on Dame Street, above the milkshake shop.'

'Are you sure that's OK?'

'Is it cool if Jacki comes over here, Sash?'

'Of course, no problem,' I could hear Sasha answer in the background.

'Thanks,' I said. 'I'll be there in a few minutes.'

I rushed through Temple Bar, past the Central Bank, and waited for the traffic lights to change. I still felt sick. The after-effects of the curse pulsed through my veins. I wanted nothing more than to go home and sleep, but that wasn't an option. I needed to figure out who'd tried to kill me, and who'd succeeded in killing Kayla.

I made my way towards the milkshake shop and pressed the buzzer for number 4.

'Come on up!' said Sasha's voice on the other end. I pushed the door open. I wasn't expecting any revelations from them, but I did think they could help me on my way to solving this.

Sasha appeared at the top of the stairs.

'Hi,' I said.

'Hey!' she said. 'We're watching movies! You missed *Juno*, but *Blue Valentine*'s just about to start.' She sounded a bit tipsy. I climbed the stairs and followed her into the apartment. It was open-plan with wooden floors and slick furniture. Ellie was sitting cross-legged on a huge cream sofa, a bowl of popcorn in her lap and an empty bottle of wine on the table in front of her.

'Hi, Jacki,' she said.

'Oh my god, Ryan Gosling is hot,' said Sasha. She ran

over to the couch and jumped on to it, then patted the seat beside her. 'Sit,' she said. 'It's starting.'

'Actually, I was hoping we could watch something else,' I said, rooting in my bag. I hated to ruin their film night, but I had a feeling they'd be able to help me. 'This might sound a bit weird,' I said, 'but I have a video from Kayla's party, of the guests, and I was wondering if you could tell me who was going out with who?'

'You have a video from Kayla's party?' said Sasha, her eyes widening.

Ellie looked surprised too.

'It's a video of her eighteen kisses,' I said. 'I've watched it myself lots of times, but I need to get more of a feel for the dynamic of the group. I understand there were a few couples in the video?'

'Yeah,' said Ellie. 'I guess there were a few . . . but why would you need to know something like that?'

'I want to find out as much about the party as possible,' I said. 'To help me figure out what might have happened.'

'Fair enough,' said Sasha. 'Put it on.'

I opened the DVD player, took out the disc that was already there, and put mine in. I pressed Play. Sasha and Ellie were silent at first, their eyes glued to Kayla, and I could tell it was upsetting for them to watch. 'I Kissed a Girl' blasted from the speakers. Kayla walked over to the stool; she fixed the strap of her dress. I knew this video so well.

'Have you seen this before?' I asked them.

'No . . .' said Ellie. 'Nobody put any photos or videos up online after the party – it didn't seem right. Except for the picture of Kayla in her dress. That ended up everywhere.'

'So,' I said, taking out my notebook and pen from my bag. 'Were any of the people in the video going out with each other?'

'Well, let's see,' said Sasha, flicking her hair back and pointing at the people on the screen. 'Libby and Rob, obviously; Amy and Andrew; Kayla and Luke were supposedly doing it behind everyone's back; oh, and Ellie and Sean,' she said, winking at Ellie. 'I think that's it.'

'Biggest mistake of my life,' muttered Ellie.

'What about before the party – had any of them previously gone out with each other, but were broken up?'

'Um, I think Rory and Libby went out for a while,' said Ellie. 'And I went out with Rob for a year. Kayla went out with Kev. That's it, I think. Calum has been with pretty much every girl in the video, but he's never actually been on a date.'

'Thanks,' I said, after I'd jotted down everything she'd said.

'You look kind of pale,' said Sasha. 'Are you OK?'

'Yeah,' I said. 'I'm just really tired.'

I decided I was going to go home and get some sleep. I wanted to stay awake, but I didn't think my body would be able to handle it.

'Thanks, guys,' I said. 'I better head off.'

As soon as I got on the bus, I examined the list of couples. I crossed off all the people who had a solid alibi. I was still left with the same pair that kept cropping up. Amy and Andrew.

Chapter 23

The next day I got up early and headed into the city centre. I had a feeling Amy was hiding something, and even though I'd thought Andrew was telling the truth about how he got Kayla's picture on his phone, there was still something suspicious about why he had kept it. I was sure I was on the right track. I'd finally have something to tell Detective Sergeant Lawlor. But first I was going to talk to Amy myself. Out of the two of them, I knew she'd be the easiest to crack. I'd have to meet her on her own, and soon. I didn't want her conferring with Andrew.

I felt much better by now. I'd woken up feeling relatively normal – no thumping headache or sick stomach. I was still utterly confused about Nick and Dillon, of course, but I tried not to think too much about that.

I arrived in Temple Bar and called Amy.

'Hi,' I said. 'It's Jacki. I'd like to talk to you. Can you come and meet me?'

'Hey, I'm just doing some shopping, and I'm in work tomorrow, but I can meet you on –'

'Amy, I really need to talk to you.'

The line went silent.

'Amy?'

'OK,' she said. I sensed panic in her voice. 'I can meet you at the ice-cream place in half an hour.'

I ordered a hot chocolate and sat at one of the tables outside. There were lots of Saturday shoppers around, browsing in the windows of the thrift stores and the shoe shops. This was due to be my second last day in Dublin. If I'd actually managed to solve the case, then I'd be packing up my stuff and getting on a bus to Avarna tomorrow. Detective Sergeant Lawlor would see to everything else after I told him who I thought the murderer was. I was looking forward to proving him right in front of Detective Sergeant Lonergan. Proving that his faith in me hadn't been misguided. I was also looking forward to going back. There was a chance that Nick might actually talk to me if I was there. I wanted to see him. Whatever ended up happening between the two of us, I felt like we needed to talk and sort the situation out. I didn't want things to end nastily like they had with Cian.

As far as Kayla was concerned, I was pretty sure I was on the right track. I could imagine Andrew might have been the one to kill her, but if it was him I couldn't understand why Amy was still covering for him. But then again, like Ger had said, you'd be surprised at the lengths people will go to to protect the ones they love. Maybe Amy had been so in love with him that she'd decided to lie, and now she was too afraid to go back on it?

Soon after that, Amy appeared, dropped her shopping bags on the ground and sitting down across from me. I was glad we were meeting in a public place. When I confronted her, she wouldn't be able to hurt me. Not that I was scared of her. Judging by how I assumed she'd used Lauren, she probably got other people to do all her dirty work for her.

'I don't think you've been entirely truthful with me,' I said. 'Have you?'

She started to cry. A couple sitting two tables away glanced over, but then resumed sharing their ice cream.

'Please stop crying, Amy,' I said. 'I think I know what really happened. It will be easier if you just tell me in your own words.'

She just kept sobbing.

'Amy?' I pushed gently.

'OK!' she said. ' I'm sorry, you're right. I admit it. I didn't walk her to the top of the laneway. I fought with Andrew outside the supermarket, and Kayla said she had to get back to the party. I let her start walking by herself. Then Andrew and I made up, and I said we had to go and catch up with her. He wanted us to go to his house instead, and that was in the other direction. I was determined to stay on his good side, but I also wanted to walk Kayla home – I didn't want people to think I'd left her alone on her birthday. I remember exactly what Andrew whispered to me. He said, "Just say you walked her home – it's not like she's going to remember." I was so relieved we'd made up, I decided to go with him.

'So I texted Kayla and said I had a headache and was going home. I never heard back from her; I just assumed she was mad at me. The next morning, when Hazel called, I said

I'd walked her to the top of the road. It just automatically came out. I was scared to change my story, scared to go back. Andrew has a criminal record – he beat up a guy in a nightclub once – so I didn't want to draw any attention to him. I just felt like I couldn't backtrack. It was too late; we'd already lied. I didn't see what difference a few minutes' walk would make; I thought she'd just gone off somewhere and would turn up . . .'

I was confused. This wasn't the confession I was expecting from Amy. What about the part where Andrew had taken her? Had Amy not even seen that happen? Had he gone back after Kayla at some point?

'Amy, tell me the whole story. Do you think Andrew might have hurt her? Is that why you didn't want to draw attention to him?'

'No! God, no! I was with him the whole time – he never left my side that night. You know what people are like if you've got a criminal record. I didn't want to go to the guards and tell them I'd lied. Andrew was so temperamental at that stage. I didn't see what a mistake the relationship was – I just felt like I needed him to survive. And I'd told the story so many times – how I'd walked her to the top of the road, how I'd hugged her goodbye, that I started to believe it myself.'

'But what did Andrew do to her? What do you know that you're not telling me? You don't have to cover for him any more. Or was it you? Did you hurt her?'

'Jacki, I didn't hurt her! I can't help thinking if I'd walked her that extra bit more that she'd have got home OK. But Andrew said she could just as easily have been taken from her own road. God, you can't think I would hurt her. I'd never do that.'

'But you paid Lauren to get rid of me.'

'What? Lauren O'Keefe? I haven't talked to Lauren properly in years. What do you mean I *paid her to get rid of you*? There's nobody that wants you here more than me, Jacki. There's nobody who wants Kayla to be found more than me.'

I was floored by this – if Amy was lying, she was doing a very good job of it. I didn't know whether to believe her now or not.

'What did you fight about?' I asked. 'You and Andrew?'

'Well, you see, Kayla was looking at this magazine in the shop – *Electric* magazine I think it was called. It was the latest issue just out, and it had a collection of their best music photography in it. Bruce Springsteen was on the cover, I remember, because Andrew started singing "Born in the USA" very loudly, and the cashier was looking at us disapprovingly. Kayla was going to buy it, but Andrew offered to buy it for her, kind of as a birthday present. Listen, I'm not proud of this, but basically I went mental. They used to go out and I was always jealous of her. Even though they'd only gone out for, like, a week or something, I knew he'd been in love with her for ages, and I'd always thought of myself as his second choice. He never did things like that for me, like spontaneously buying me stuff. And I saw how grateful she was and it just triggered something inside me and I sort of flipped. Kayla went off to find the marshmallows and Andrew and I were fighting in the magazine aisle, and then again outside, whispering back and forth so that Kayla wouldn't hear what we were fighting about. But I think she knew anyway. She said she had to get back to the party, that she'd meet us there. We basically made her feel so awkward that she left.'

I thought back to last week, when I'd gone into Kayla's room. I remembered the doll's house and the camera equipment and the Polaroids, but most importantly I remembered the bookshelf, with the photography books and the poetry collections, and the stack of *Electric* magazines. I could have sworn the one on the top had a cover showing Bruce Springsteen. But I wasn't entirely sure.

'Did Andrew give her the magazine?' I asked.

'Yeah, he bought it for her.'

'No, did he give it to her, did she have it with her before heading back to the party?'

'Yeah, yeah, she did.'

If she had gone back to the party, maybe something had happened to her right inside the house. I'd felt really dizzy walking up the spiral stairs to her bedroom; maybe something had happened up there. I wasn't absolutely certain that I'd seen the magazine in her room though. I had to check.

'Thanks, Amy,' I said. 'I'm sorry to make you go over this, but I may have to talk to you again.'

'It's okay,' she said. I felt her eyes watching me sadly as I left.

I went to George's Street Arcade to retrieve Kayla's necklace from Lauren. I made sure she swore it was safe before I took it. I wanted to go to Kayla's house, but I didn't want to turn up without a reason. I'd already seen her room once; I wasn't sure if I'd be allowed to see it again, especially if her parents were back.

As I walked up Sycamore Road, I examined the necklace. The tips of the star pendant were discoloured from where it had scalded Lauren's hands. I really hoped nobody would notice. I'd promised to take good care of it, and now I was returning it in this state. You had to look at it really closely to notice the damage though, and there was nothing I could do about it now.

A woman with a blonde bob opened the door. She looked a lot like Kayla, so I assumed it was her mum.

'Anna?' I asked. 'I'm Jacki, I'm helping Detective Sergeant Lawlor.'

'Oh yes, of course. Come in,' she said.

I stepped into the hallway.

'I wanted to return Kayla's necklace,' I said.

'Was it of any help?' she asked.

'I'm not sure . . . I'm afraid I've nothing conclusive yet. But I'd also like to see her room once more,' I said. 'If that's possible?'

'Yes, of course,' she said. 'Come with me.' She was a lot more accommodating than I'd expected her to be. Much like Libby, I suppose.

I followed her up the stairs and along the corridor, then up the spiral staircase. I pretended to look around the room, not wanting to dart directly to the bookshelf. Even though I was desperate to examine it, I didn't want to seem suspicious. I wanted it to look like I was trying to connect with Kayla, not that I was searching for something in particular. I moved slowly towards the shelf. Sure enough, there it was.

On top of the pile of magazines was the issue with Bruce Springsteen on the cover. Kayla had come back here after all. My heart started to race.

'Every time I look at these Polaroids I spot something new,' said Anna.

I turned round. 'They're beautiful.'

'Like that one,' said Anna, pointing to the photo of the white butterfly landing on the purple thistle.

'Yes,' I said. 'I noticed that one the last time I was here.'

'Ah, but did you notice everything about it?' she asked.

'Sorry?'

'Take a closer look.'

I walked towards the photograph. I stared at it, but didn't immediately notice anything new. However, after a few more moments, I saw it. A small brown snail, blending in with the darkest part of the thistle.

'That photograph won a competition,' said Anna. 'So few people notice the snail at first. They're so fixated on the butterfly that they don't even think to look for anything else.'

I froze at Anna's words. Suddenly I knew what I had to do.

I ran to the bus stop and frantically looked through my bag, finally deciding to tip the contents out on to the ground. It wasn't there though. I must have left it at Ellie and Sasha's.

'Crap,' I muttered. I ran through the square, all the way to their house, and pressed the buzzer. *Please be here, please be here.*

'Hello?'

'Sasha, it's Jacki.'

'Hey, Jacki,' she said as she released the door.

'I think I left my DVD here,' I gasped.

'Oh, right, come on up and check, if you like.'

'Thanks.'

I clambered up the stairs. Sasha opened the door. I thanked her and ran straight for the DVD player. I wanted to watch the video again. It had to hold the answer. The killer or killers were at the party; they must have been in the video. I'd watched it over and over, but maybe I was missing something. I had to be missing something. Kayla had made it back to the house; she'd brought the magazine up to her room. Calum was right: he had seen her.

'Um, Sasha,' I said. 'Do you mind if I watch this again?'

'Fire away,' she said, sitting down on the couch and opening her textbook.

Once again I watched Kayla sitting on the chair. I watched her being kissed by everyone – Rob, Amy, Andrew, Libby, Hazel, Kev, Sasha, Ellie . . .

Then I saw something blocking the bottom right-hand corner. It was there for a second, and then it was gone. I knelt down and rewound the DVD. But when I played it again I realized it was just somebody's thumb, the thumb that belonged to whoever had taken the video. My heart started to pound. I remembered Matt's words on the day we'd met in Ming's. *I strongly suspect that her killer is in this video.* All the times I'd watched this I hadn't spotted what was right in front of me. It was like the snail beside the butterfly. I'd been concentrating so hard on the obvious that I hadn't been looking for anything else.

'Sasha?'

'Yeah?'

'Do you remember who took this?'

'Hmm?' she said, looking up from her book.

'Who was holding the video camera? At Kayla's party?'

'Ooh, let me think . . . Actually, I do remember, because I kept telling him to stop getting my side profile, but he wouldn't listen.'

'Who was it?'

'Hazel's boyfriend. Barry.'

Chapter 24

I walked through Temple Bar Square, pushing my way past shoppers and buskers. I remembered Hazel handing me back the necklace. She must have given it to Lauren that night and asked her to curse it. It was only after the gig that I'd started to feel really horrible. I'd assumed it was just because I was heartbroken at the time, but now I knew that I was also being psychically attacked. And I couldn't believe it – Hazel had given me Andrew's phone to try and throw me off course. Detective Sergeant Lawlor was right, the killer *was* in the video, he just wasn't on my list. Hazel knew, that's why she'd given me the necklace – she was covering up for Barry. How could she do that? Kayla was her half-sister! Maybe she was afraid to come forward, to say she'd lied? I didn't get it. I didn't understand it at all. I looked down at my elbow. The scratch was fading, a sign that I was nearly there, perhaps, that I was on the right track.

Rage looked different now that I was so angry, now that I knew what Hazel had done. Faded grubby stains showed up on the furniture and the plectrum-paved floor seemed cheap, almost tacky. There was nobody there, apart from

Hazel, who was sitting at a table in the middle of the floor. She was wearing a ripped Rolling Stones T-shirt, huge fake eyelashes and deep red lipstick. There were lots of sheets of paper scattered in front of her.

'Hey, hun,' she said as I closed the door behind me. 'What's up?'

I didn't answer. She surveyed my face and I saw realization spread slowly across hers. There was a silent understanding – she knew I was on to her. I could feel the sudden tension between us, a heavy hesitation in the air. I took a deep breath.

'Would you like a drink?' she said. 'We're not actually open yet, but I can get you a –'

'I don't want a drink,' I said, walking towards her. 'I know what happened.'

'Excuse me?' she said, playing dumb. The question seemed more of a reflex though. It lacked any real conviction. This was it. She'd been found out and she knew it.

'I know you paid Lauren to curse me,' I said flatly. 'I know Barry killed Kayla. I know he buried her in the mountains.' I looked straight at her, but she avoided my stare, instead collecting the sheets of paper into a neat pile.

'Well, two out of three ain't bad, I suppose,' she said, without looking up. 'I had a feeling you'd be visiting me soon.' She raised her head and smiled. 'You just wouldn't go away,' she said, angrily punctuating each word. She tapped the pile of sheets against the table and slid a paper clip across the top. 'I had to prepare,' she said. 'I knew it was possible you'd figure things out eventually. Well, almost figure things out.'

I gave her a questioning look.

'Barry didn't kill her,' she said.

I couldn't believe she was continuing to deny it.

'Of course you'd say that,' I replied.

'I'm telling the truth,' said Hazel, looking straight at me.

'Well then, who was it?' I moved closer to her. 'Do you know?'

'Of course I know,' she said and smiled.

I tried to think. I was right about the curse, I was right about Barry, but was I wrong about the fact that a couple had been involved in the murder? Had Lauren led me astray? I'd been so sure that she was telling the truth. And then it hit me. I felt sick. Was it possible that I'd just walked straight into Hazel's trap? That's why she didn't want to come forward. She wasn't covering up for Barry – *he was covering up for her*.

Hazel killed Kayla.

I was in total disbelief. How could she do that? How could she kill her own half-sister? I looked around me, suddenly quite afraid. Nobody knew I was here. I could be in danger. But I needed to know everything that had happened. There would be no point in leaving here and not being able to prove anything. I decided to keep her calm, keep her talking.

'You have her name tattooed on your wrist,' I said. 'How can you have the person you murdered tattooed on your wrist?'

Hazel smirked. 'I didn't kill her,' she said. I rolled my eyes. I couldn't believe she was actually trying to deny it.

'Seriously,' she said, signalling for me to have a seat. I

ignored her offer. I needed to stay on my feet. In case I had to run.

'I didn't kill her,' she said flatly. 'Libby did.'

I let out an unconvinced laugh, but she stared back at me so genuinely that I had to sit down. Everything started to slot together in my mind, everything gradually, but definitely becoming clearer. I remembered the first time I'd met Libby, how she'd defended Amy, saying that people shouldn't blame her. Was she actually defending herself? She was the one who'd given me the necklace in the first place and Matt had been surprised at her willingness. I'd thought it was because she trusted me, but was it actually because she wanted to get rid of me? Had they been planning the attack all along? But why had she done it? Had she really hated Kayla that much? And why was Hazel covering for her?

'She didn't do it on purpose,' said Hazel, as if reading my thoughts. 'The night of the party, Kayla came back from the shop and went straight upstairs. She walked in on Libby rooting through her stuff.'

'So she did come back to the house,' I said.

'Yeah. Nobody else saw her come in though,' said Hazel.

'Calum said he thought he saw her . . . and he wasn't lying.'

'Calum was hammered; nobody really believed him and he wasn't even sure himself anyway.'

'Why was Libby going through her stuff?' I asked.

'She was convinced Kayla had hidden her pills, and she was right.'

'So, what, Libby killed Kayla because she'd hidden her drugs?'

'Kayla hadn't hidden them out of any sisterly affection,' said Hazel coldly. 'She just didn't want Libby getting off her face, or offering them to any of her angelic friends. Just because Kayla didn't agree with it didn't mean she had the right to control everybody else. Libby worked hard; she deserved to let loose once in a while. Anyway, Libby found them hidden in Kayla's room and went mental. And she told Kayla to stay away from her boyfriend too, that she obviously liked him, but that he wasn't interested and it just made Kayla look pathetic. Everybody knew Rob liked Kayla, and it tore Libby apart. And then Kayla said something like, "I don't want to steal him, but I could if I wanted to." And she pushed past Libby to get to her mirror. That was too much. Libby just snapped; she pushed Kayla back too hard and she went tumbling down the stairs. Libby said she could hear the crack of her neck as she hit the floor. She wanted to call for somebody, she wanted to explain what had happened, but she said her body just shut down and she wasn't able to cope with the situation. The guilt was too much and she wasn't able to move. That can happen – you just completely go into shock. I went upstairs to go to the bathroom and found Libby hunched over on the floor, facing away from Kayla and just muttering, "Oh my god, oh my god, oh my god." I knew before I touched Kayla that she was dead; I could sense it. She wasn't breathing; she was definitely gone and there was nothing I could do for her. I looked at Libby, and I was about to call an ambulance, but then I could hear my mum's voice in my head: *"Take care of your little sister."* And I guess this sort of weird protective urge kicked in, and I knew I could do something. I knew Libby's life didn't have to be ruined. She could claim it was an accident or self-defence or whatever, but everybody knew they hated each other. Libby wanted to be a doctor; she couldn't get a criminal record. Kayla was already dead, there was nothing I could do for her, but I could save Libby.'

'Your mother wouldn't have wanted you to lie,' I said.

'You don't have any siblings, do you?' she asked. I didn't answer. I didn't want to tell her that my mum was expecting a baby, that I was going to have a little brother or sister. I didn't want her to know something like that.

'If you did, you might be able to understand.'

'I know I wouldn't help cover up something like this.'

'Really?' she said. 'We'd all like to think we'd do the right thing, but I don't think you can be sure what you'd do until the time comes to make the decision. It's easy for you to sit there and judge me and tell me what I should have done. Do you not think I deeply regret everything that's happened? Of course I do. Of course I see Kayla's face every time I close my eyes; of course I think I hear her speak to me in that house when I'm trying to sleep. But it's done now. I made a decision and I have to deal with it. And I still think Libby is better off this way. I still think it was the right choice.'

In a way I felt sorry for Libby. She was living with this horrible guilt and secrecy, but she didn't have to. It had been Hazel's idea to cover it up, not Libby's. She'd only gone along with it. Hazel had convinced her to do it – and she'd convinced Barry to bury Kayla.

'And you didn't mind dragging your boyfriend into it too?' I said.

Hazel smiled.

'Barry's in the army,' she said. 'He's seen a lot worse than that. I knew I couldn't get rid of the body by myself, and Libby was in no state to help me. It was difficult to think, what with all the noise coming from downstairs, but I came up with a plan. I told Libby to put some make-up on and go downstairs and act like nothing was wrong. If she was gone much longer, people would start to get suspicious. I told her that the first few hours would be the worst, that once she got past them she'd be able to cope. Because I figured once you go far enough into a lie you're too scared to go back anyway. She was hysterical, but I kept telling her to calm down and not to tell anyone. It was really important not to tell anyone.

'Those initial hours *were* the worst. I knew if I could get her through them then everything would be all right. It took me a while, but I eventually calmed her down. I explained the situation to Barry – it took a bit of convincing, but he's so in love with me that he agreed. I reminded him that he told me he'd do anything for me, and that I'd owe him so much if he did this. I knew I could trust him to keep a secret. I didn't want to get rid of the body that night because I knew we'd have to find somewhere really remote. So we put her in a black bin bag and hid her in Barry's garage. I kept watch while he was moving her. Nobody noticed. I asked him to cut up the body – I wanted to hide it in different places so it would be harder to find, and he tried, but he only barely cut her arm before he gave up. He wasn't able to do it; he wasn't as strong as I'd thought. That nearly broke him – he was going to call the guards then.'

I looked down at the faded scratch on my arm that ran right round my elbow and I felt disgust rise inside me.

'Why didn't you do it yourself?' I said. 'If you wanted her cut up, why didn't *you* do it?'

'You think I couldn't have, don't you? You think I'm a coward.'

I didn't answer. I didn't think she was a coward – I was afraid of what she was capable of. She was clearly completely unstable and dangerous.

'I could have,' she said. 'But you see, so far, I hadn't done anything. I didn't want Libby to go to jail, but I sure as hell wasn't going in her place. I could have buried Kayla myself, but I wanted Barry to do it. I told him I'd do anything. I think he liked that. I don't think he ever felt like he was in control in our relationship, and this gave him the dominance he wanted. It all just worked out. Libby and I, we acted like everything was normal, and we pretended to be worried about her just like everybody else. And it got easier with time. That serial killer was going around abducting women, conveniently enough, and people just jumped to that conclusion. Nobody suspected any of us.'

'Detective Sergeant Lawlor did,' I said.

'Yes, well, he's special, isn't he? Very special, in fact,' she smirked.

I ignored her. I couldn't believe she was being so obnoxious while confessing to what she'd done.

'Do . . . Anna and your father know?' I asked. I couldn't imagine they'd help cover for them like this, but I guessed anything was possible.

'No. I've thought about telling Dad, but he's too in love with Anna. He'd want to tell her. The only people who know are me, Libby and Barry. And you. That's it. Barry won't tell anybody. He knows he'd go to jail.

'It feels good to tell somebody all this,' Hazel added with a sigh. 'I've been holding it in for so long.'

'I'm glad you told me,' I said, starting to back away. I had all the information I came for. 'It must be a relief to get it off your chest. And when we tell the guards that will be an even bigger relief. Libby is a nervous wreck – she needs to tell somebody.'

'Libby was fine before all this was dragged up. And she'll be fine again, now that everything has been taken care of.'

'What do you mean?'

'This isn't getting out,' said Hazel, walking over to the door and locking it. I was starting to feel kind of scared now. I was ready for a fight, but I had no idea what this girl might try to do.

'Detective Sergeant Lawlor's outside,' I said confidently.

She laughed. 'Sure he is. Don't worry though, I'm not going to hurt you. Take a seat – I have something you might like to see.'

I decided to stay. I wanted to see, I wanted to know.

Hazel walked behind the bar and re-emerged with a laptop. She opened it up.

What was she going to show me? I wondered. I had no idea.

Hazel switched on the laptop and waited for it to power up.

'Mum asked me to take care of Libby,' she said, staring at it.

'She said, "Hazel, please look after your sister. Keep her safe, no matter what it takes."'

She opened the photo application and clicked on one photo so that it zoomed out, taking up the entire screen. It was a picture of Hazel kissing some guy.

'Why are you showing me th–' I suddenly recognized who it was . . . Matt Lawlor. Detective Sergeant Lawlor.

'I don't think Matt'd like his boss to see this,' she said. 'Or his partner, for that matter.'

Oh my god. What had he done? I couldn't believe it. No wonder Matt had wanted me on the case. It wasn't only my ability to communicate with the dead that he needed – he knew he'd compromised the integrity of the investigation and he needed someone untainted – like me – to finish what he had started. I thought back to how he'd seemed reluctant to commit to any further cases. He'd said, '*We'll see what happens*.' He must have known this might come out. He knew that this might mean the end of his career if Hazel decided to blackmail him.

'You won't get away with it,' I said.

'The case has been jeopardized,' said Hazel. 'I'm sure the police will agree to step back on the condition that I keep this under wraps.'

'No. Detective Sergeant Lawlor –' I stopped. I didn't want Hazel knowing Matt was probably prepared to sacrifice himself for the good of this investigation. I needed her to think she was going to get away with it.

'If this gets out, the case is jeopardized and Matt loses his job. If this doesn't get out, the case still doesn't get solved, but Matt doesn't lose his job. Everybody wins.'

I was getting angrier by the second.

'This was a last resort, of course,' she said. 'But you just wouldn't go away. I did what I needed to do. Anyone would have done the same.' She pointed to the photo, her sleeve falling back, exposing her tattoo. 'I got there in the end.'

'You have her name on your arm,' I said again in disbelief.

'I still love her, you know. But I love Libby more.'

I couldn't believe she'd done this. With Amy and Lauren, there was panic in their voices, and regret. Sure, they'd done deceitful things, but they were ashamed. Hazel just stood there with this smug look on her face. I know she wanted to protect her sister, but I think she enjoyed doing it. I think she got some sort of sick thrill out of this, ripping apart people's lives and watching the world decay around her. She must have seen what this did to Amy, what it did to Lauren. She'd handed me that necklace, knowing it could have killed me.

'I'm going to get away with this, Jacki. You just have to accept it. I know it's frustrating. Here, take a copy,' she said, ejecting the disc and handing it to me. 'I've got plenty.'

I took it from her and then I flung it across the floor. I wanted to pick up the laptop and fling it across the floor too. I wanted to scream and tear the frames off the walls, smash her perfectly constructed face in, but what was the point?

'Open the door,' I said.

She swung it open lazily. 'I'm sorry it had to end like this. But I had no choice.'

'You're not sorry.'

'No, you're right. Perhaps I will be in the next life,' said Hazel as I walked away. 'But not in this one.'

Chapter 25

That night I went to sleep in my bed at Gran's, but I didn't dream about the car and the Polaroid camera and the barbed-wire fence. Instead I saw what happened to Kayla.

I watched her go into her room. Libby was bending down on the floor beside the doll's house, its tiny wooden furniture all sprawled across the carpet. She was wearing a tight black dress and her hair was styled in loose curls. Her shoes were silver and sky high. She turned round and held up a small plastic packet of pills.

'I knew you hid them,' she said. 'What the hell is your problem?'

'You shouldn't take those,' said Kayla, sounding upset. 'You don't need to.'

'What I don't need is you poking around in my business,' said Libby, standing up and adjusting her dress. 'Stay out of it! And stay away from Rob too. *Stop* flirting with him. It just makes you look pathetic; you're never going to have him.'

'I wasn't flirting with him,' said Kayla. 'I told him ages ago that I wasn't interested. I don't like him at all.'

'You're a liar,' said Libby.

'I don't want to talk about this any more,' said Kayla, pushing past Libby to get to her mirror. 'I don't want to steal him, but just so you know, I could if I wanted to.'

Libby shoved her hard. Kayla was unsteady on her stilettos, then she stumbled backwards. Libby suddenly looked scared and reached out her hand to try and grab Kayla, but it was too late. She went toppling down the spiral staircase. Then I heard a crack.

'Oh my god,' whispered Libby in horror.

She rushed down after Kayla, holding on to both banisters to steady herself.

'Kayla, are you OK?' she asked frantically. She shook her, but Kayla didn't move. Libby hunched down on the ground and just kept muttering, 'Oh my god, oh my god, oh my god.'

I could see Hazel walking down the corridor towards them. She was wearing ripped black jeans, a purple top and black leather ankle boots. She spotted Libby first.

'Get up, you drunken mess,' she said with a laugh, but stopped dead when she saw Kayla. She hurried over and knelt beside her, the colour draining slowly from her face.

'What did you do?' said Hazel.

'I'm so sorry,' whimpered Libby. 'It was an accident. I didn't mean to –'

'What happened?'

'I . . . I pushed her,' she said, '. . . down the stairs.'

Hazel's eyes widened.

'We were having a fight because I was in her room. She pushed me first, but I . . . I pushed her too hard. I'm so sorry, I'm so, so sorry.'

'Did anybody else see this?' asked Hazel.

'No,' said Libby.

Hazel grabbed Kayla's arms and dragged her body into one of the bedrooms. Then she came back out, closing the door quietly behind her.

'Go into your room, fix your make-up and pretend nothing happened,' she said. 'Do you hear me?'

'What are you talking about?' said Libby, suddenly snapping out of her trance. 'We have to call an ambulance.'

'She's dead, Libby.'

'No . . . she, she can't be, we need to call an ambulance!'

'I told Mum I'd look after you,' said Hazel. 'Do you want to go to jail?'

'Hazel, we have to call somebody!'

'*Libby, do you want to go to jail?*'

'No,' she sobbed.

'Then go put on your make-up.'

The scene quickly changed and then rain was crashing against the windscreen. A guy was driving and Hazel was sitting in the passenger seat.

'Here?' he said.

'No. It has to be somewhere really secluded.'

'Do you think anybody saw us?'

'Nobody saw us. Can we just concentrate on finding a place to bury her?'

There was silence then, apart from the weather report on the radio, forecasting more rain.

'Do you even know where we're going?' he said.

'Away from any houses.'

They drove for a few more minutes, neither of them talking. Hazel turned up the radio.

'*Welcome to two hours of non-stop alternative rock!*'

'Pictures of You' started to play.

'Oh god,' said Barry. 'That was her favourite song, wasn't it?'

'Um . . . I dunno,' said Hazel.

'It was,' he said. 'I remember her saying it before. What if it's her way of telling us something . . . letting us know that we won't get away with it?'

'Listen to yourself, Barry. I've never heard anything more ridiculous in my life.'

'Yeah,' he said, taking a deep breath. 'You're right. Sorry, babe, this whole thing is making me go insane.'

'It's OK,' she said, rubbing his arm. 'Don't worry, it's nearly over.'

He opened the door.

'Don't forget this,' said Hazel, handing him the balaclava. He pulled it on over his head and got out of the car.

Hazel quickly turned off the radio.

I woke up shaking and sweating, but an enormous relief came over me. I knew what I had to do. I had to tell the Gardai everything I knew. After I'd done that I wouldn't be dreaming about her any more.

The next day I found myself once again walking down Grafton Street on a Sunday morning. I still hadn't heard from Nick – or Colin, who was obviously still furious at me for our last fight. He was going to New York soon so it would be even longer before we spoke . . . if he ever planned to speak to me again. At least I was beginning to feel OK about Nick though. Hannah had been right – things had started to become gradually more and more normal again. And more and more, my thoughts kept turning back to Dillon. I smiled – would he really wait those eighty-four days? I wasn't so sure, but it made me happy thinking about the fun we'd had.

Because I'd spent the last day of term at *Electric* magazine and not in class, I had to keep reminding myself that school was actually over, that I was free for the rest of the summer. I planned to spend my first days of freedom doing nothing at all. After the stress of the past few weeks I was looking forward to relaxing.

It had been really hard confronting Matt Lawlor and handing him the disc with the photograph. He knew what was on it before he'd even opened it. I could see the shame in his eyes.

'You've done the right thing, Jacki,' he said. 'I'm so sorry that I let you down like this, but you see now why I needed you on this case. It wasn't just your incredible psychic sense that let you see things no one else could, but your impartiality also meant that you would see this through – even when I couldn't. I'd begun to have my suspicions about Hazel. I had a feeling that she might be covering up for somebody, but I couldn't do anything, not when I'd been involved with her. I'm going to tell the team everything now. I'm going to make this right.'

I'd left devastated. In some ways Hazel had won – Detective Sergeant Lawlor would probably lose his job, even though by confessing, he thought they might be able to save the case and secure a conviction that would send her to prison where she belonged. If he did, then that would probably mean the end of me working on the operation. I felt so sorry for him – I knew he hadn't meant for this to happen. I thought it incredibly careless that he had got involved with Kayla's half-sister, but I didn't want him to lose his career over it. And although my time working on this case had been stressful and dangerous, I hated to think that this was the end.

And so I had absolutely no idea why Matt had texted, asking me to meet him in Ming's today. He couldn't want to go over everything again, surely? Maybe he had been officially let go from the Gardai now and wanted to tell me in person. Something didn't quite add up though.

I arrived at the window of the restaurant and saw the three of them sitting inside, all wearing suits. Matt's collar was unbuttoned and he looked scruffy and unshaven. Sergeant Ray Harte looked tired and Detective Sergeant Tony Lonergan just looked annoyed.

Matt was the first to spot me. I tried to read his face for clues, for a sign as to how he thought this meeting might unfold, but he wasn't giving anything away. I tried to stay positive – I really hoped Hazel wasn't going to win. I held the handle of my satchel a little tighter, then headed inside. Just like last time, there was nobody else there – it was only the four of us. I ordered a hot chocolate and joined them.

'Hello,' said Matt as I sat down at the table, giving me a meek smile. Ray nodded amicably in my direction.

'Hello, Jacki,' said Tony. 'Glad you could make it.'

Maybe I'd imagined it, but his voice actually sounded sincere.

We sat in silence for a few minutes and I wondered what they were waiting for. Then the waitress came over and placed my drink in front of me, and I realized they were making sure we weren't overheard. As soon as she'd left, Tony started to speak.

'I'm sure I don't need to explain to any of you the seriousness of the situation,' he said.

Matt stared into his cup of coffee.

'It's very unfortunate,' Tony continued. 'But it doesn't have to destroy this operation. I've decided that it will go no further. From now on, that photo doesn't exist. Ray will take care of it.'

I looked over at Matt. He nodded. It was obvious he had been told this before, but was still too deeply ashamed to be properly happy. I couldn't believe it. Detective Sergeant Lonergan had decided to help keep him on the team.

'We need you to agree that this will go no further, Jacki. The case and the integrity of this operation depends on it.'

'Of course!' I stammered.

'Then I also owe you an apology for doubting the very special skills you brought to this case.'

'Thank you.' I hadn't expected that at all. Matt looked at me proudly from the other side of the table. 'Does this mean you're going to arrest Hazel, Barry and Libby?' I asked quietly.

'Yes,' answered Ray. 'Libby will be charged with manslaughter, and Hazel and Barry are accessories after the fact because they helped cover up the crime. That's also a very serious offence.'

I was so relieved. It felt like such a weight had been lifted off my shoulders. I took a sip from my hot chocolate.

'Right, we better get to work,' said Tony. He and Ray stood up to leave, but Matt stayed.

'Detective Sergeant Lawlor has one last thing to give to you regarding the case, Jacki.'

They left, and it was just me and Matt. I looked at him, confused. Why would I need any more information from the case? It was all closed now, wasn't it? At least I hoped it was.

He leaned down to a bag that was sitting next to his chair and pulled out a brown envelope. 'There was a thousand-euro reward attached to the case for information,' he said. 'We want you to have it – you saved it for everyone, after all.'

'That's not why I took on the case, Matt. I didn't even know that a reward existed – you must know that.' It didn't feel right to take the money.

Matt finished his cup of tea. 'You know,' he said, 'when I first heard about you, I knew you were something special. I had a feeling that you'd be perfect for this operation. Tony thought I was mad, but I was determined to prove him wrong. You deserve this, Jacki. Take it – and welcome to the team.'

I hesitated. I felt that maybe it was tainted, that whatever I used it for would only bring trouble.

'Think what you could buy with it,' said Matt. 'Is there nothing you really want?'

And then it hit me. There was something I really wanted, or rather, something I really wanted to do.

'OK,' I said. 'I accept. Thank you.'

I drank the last of my hot chocolate. 'So . . . what's next?' I asked.

'Well, you know that serial killer? The one who everybody thinks murdered Kayla?'

'Yes,' I said. 'Except we know he didn't.'

'He didn't kill Kayla,' said Matt, 'but he may be connected to some of the other cases.'

A shiver shot down my spine. The thought that there was actually a serial killer out there, kidnapping women, was almost too frightening to consider.

'Is he still abducting people?' I asked. 'Do you think he could strike again?'

'Let's just say, the sooner we catch him, the better,' Matt replied. 'I'll sleep better knowing he's off the streets.'

A family came into the diner and ordered milkshakes, the youngest daughter trying to jump up on her dad's back.

'Do you have any idea where he's from?' I whispered. 'Why he's doing it?'

'We can't talk about it here,' said Matt. 'But I'll be in touch. Very soon.'

'OK,' I said, standing up to leave. 'I'm looking forward to it.'

I rushed out of Ming's. The sun was shining now and I took off my cardigan and stuffed it in my bag. I ran up Grafton Street and just barely made it on to the tram, the door closing shut right behind me. It seemed to take forever. I willed it to go faster, checking my watch every few moments and watching the seconds ticking down. I got off at my stop and ran all the way to Gran's.

I checked the flight online and ONLY TWO SEATS LEFT flashed up on the screen. I'd have to hurry. I rushed up the stairs, found my suitcase and threw my stuff into it. I tried to remember all the essentials: phone, passport, charger, hair straightener, eyeliner . . . I sat on the suitcase and zipped it shut. The flight was leaving in less than four hours, so I had to hurry.

I left a note for Gran, explaining where I was going, then rushed out of the house and hailed a taxi. For a split second I hesitated, thinking about how much it would cost, but then I remembered it didn't matter. I had a giant wad of money in my handbag.

I called Mum from the taxi, just because my life wouldn't be worth living if I left the country without telling her. I called Colin, but his phone was turned off. I checked my watch and wished for the traffic to move more quickly.

Chapter 26

The airport was pretty busy and there were lots of people milling around the departure lounge. Some wore sun hats and bright colours and others smart business suits and serious expressions. I wove through a big group of kids in matching yellow tracksuits, then checked in my suitcase.

'Did you pack this yourself?'

I nodded, remembering the scramble to get everything ready. I wasn't even sure what was in it. I'd packed so quickly it was a complete mess. The envelope with the three remaining photographs was in there though, I was certain of that. It might have been weird to bring it on holiday, but it didn't feel right to leave it behind. It was almost overwhelming to think that I still had to help another three missing women, not to mention the fact that Matt thought a serial killer might be involved. But I was looking forward to it. Like Ger had said, a unique path had been chosen for me. I knew the journey wasn't over yet.

As I joined the queue for security, I realized how relieved I was to be leaving Ireland, even if it was just for a little while. I was sure there would be huge interest surrounding

Libby and Hazel's arrests, and I was glad I wouldn't be there for it. Even thinking about Hazel made me feel sick, so I definitely didn't want to see her face every time I turned on my TV. There was something wrong with that girl, something seriously wrong. I shuddered as I remembered sitting across from her in the bar, the indifference in her eyes as she told me everything. I didn't regret it though. Kayla had moved on, she'd found peace – that was the most important thing.

I reached the top of the queue, took off my shoes and put them in the grey box along with my handbag and jewellery and the spare change from my pocket, then placed them on the security belt.

I looked up at the screen. GO TO GATE 406 flashed beside my flight number. As I walked through the metal detector, I actually started to get excited. I'd been so busy just trying to get to the airport that it hadn't really sunk in before. I was going to New York City. A magnet for songwriting genius, the birthplace of punk rock, home of the Chelsea Hotel. I'd always imagined it as an incredibly cool place, where the music is loud and the lights are bright and anything is possible. And I was going there with my best friend in the world, even if he didn't know it yet. Luckily Colin had kept emailing me updates of the travel arrangements over the last few months, in the hope that I would eventually cave, so I knew we were going to be on the same flight.

I picked up my stuff, put my shoes back on and headed for the gate. As I power-walked down the corridor, fear started to mix in with my excitement. What if Colin was still mad at me? I wouldn't be surprised if he was. If so, it was going to be a very long trip.

'Enjoy your flight!' said the attendant as she took my boarding pass. I couldn't believe I'd actually made it. Against all odds I was on my way – I was going to be at Lydia's wedding after all. How had I thought that hanging around Avarna with Nick all summer would be better than that?

I walked up the aisle, looking out for Colin. I could hear his parents chatting, and then I saw Colin's bright red hair in the seat behind them, about halfway up the plane. I was so happy to be there, but I was also scared. I really wasn't sure what his reaction was going to be. I took my handbag off my shoulder and walked slowly towards his seat. I opened the hand-luggage compartment above his head, but he didn't look up, he was too busy talking to the woman sitting next to him.

'You see, I always try to be positive,' he said, sounding deflated. 'And although she's not even talking to me any more, I really thought it would work out. I felt it, you know? I was so sure.'

I put my bag in the compartment, moving a jacket aside so that it would fit. Colin kept talking to the woman, who was trying to read her in-flight magazine.

'Sometimes you put stuff out into the universe and it doesn't happen for a reason. Like, there's an actual explanation for it, and that's OK. But I was so sure she would be coming to New York. What's good about your best friend not coming to New York? How is that *meant to be*?'

The woman shrugged. At least it sounded like I hadn't done irreparable damage. If he was still describing me as his best friend, then maybe he'd forgiven me.

'I mean, I would have bet my life on it.' Colin went silent for a few seconds. 'Oh my god,' he said. 'I'm pretty sure I said that at some stage. I actually said I'd bet my life on it. Is there any way to take that back?'

'I'm sure you'll be fine,' said the woman, her tone suggesting she deeply regretted her choice of seat.

'I bet my life on it,' said Colin, getting even more agitated. 'And now I'm going on a transatlantic flight . . . Oh my god . . .'

'Your life jacket's under your seat,' I said.

Colin turned round slowly, spotted me and then shrieked. 'Jacki!'

He clambered out past the woman and threw his arms round me.

'How did you . . . But where did you . . . I don't understand!'

'I came into some money,' I said, when he loosened his grip. 'Unexpectedly.'

'So you're coming then? You're actually coming to New York?'

'Yep.'

'This is so exciting! I knew it. I knew you'd make it!'

'Would you like to swap seats with me?' said the woman, who must have had enough of Colin's dramatics.

'Oh, cool, thanks,' I said.

She smiled at me and I showed her where my seat was, then I sat down next to Colin.

'I'm so sorry,' I said. 'I'm so sorry for what I said.'

I hated remembering that night. I was so ashamed of how I'd acted.

'It's OK,' he said. 'People say things they regret when they're angry. I'm sorry too.'

I was so relieved, so glad that Colin wasn't going to hold it against me. As I sat beside him now, it was like we'd never even had the fight. That was the great thing about best friends, you could just go back to the way things were before. It wasn't that easy with boyfriends. You gave them something else, a part of yourself that you didn't give to other people, a part that wasn't so easy to repair when it had been taken for granted.

'How's James?' I said hesitantly.

'He's good,' said Colin. 'We're still not officially going out, but I don't mind.'

I could tell he did mind, but I didn't dare say anything about it. I wasn't going to risk upsetting him again.

'How did you afford the ticket?' asked Colin. 'Where did you get the money?'

'The Gardai,' I said.

'So you solved Kayla's murder?'

'Yeah . . . it was Libby, ' I whispered. 'Hazel helped her cover it up.'

'What the f–'

'I know, it's crazy. And it gets crazier. But I can't really talk about it here.'

'OK,' he said. 'Let's talk about New York!'

'*Welcome to Aer Lingus flight EI105 . . .*'

The seat-belt sign came on and I clipped mine closed. As

Colin happily listed off all the galleries he wanted to visit, I took my phone out to turn it off. There were two messages. The first one was from Nick. My heart started to beat rapidly. It said,

I need to talk to you.

I quickly texted him back.

About what?

I need to talk to you in person, can we meet up soon?
he texted back.

I saw the flight attendant coming down the aisle of the plane, her eyes on my phone. I realized I only had time to do one more thing – reply to Nick or read Dillon's text.

I smiled, instinctively knowing what I wanted to do – and pressed the button.

82 days and counting.

I smiled again as the flight attendant arrived at my side.

'Sorry, miss, you're going to have to turn off your phone,' she said.

'Jeez, Jacki, turn off your phone!' said Colin. 'You know I'm a nervous flyer!'

The plane began to move down the runway. Colin started humming 'New York, New York' and I hummed along with him. I was going to stop thinking about boys and I was going to stop analysing everything. I'd concentrate on music and Operation Trail and I'd have lots of fun at the wedding. Maybe it was for the best anyway, the fact that I couldn't reply to Nick now. I'd waited a whole week for that message; he could wait a few hours for my response. Dillon's text had made me happy and I deserved that after everything that had happened. I didn't know if he'd be able to hang on for seventy-nine more days – perhaps I'd lose my chance. But I wasn't going to think about that.

Last month I met eighteen people.

Now I was going to concentrate on me.

Acknowledgements

I'd like to thank: the team at Penguin Ireland, especially Michael, Patricia, Cliona and Phil. Paddy O'Doherty for her fabulous insight and editing skills. Claire Hennessy and Eimear Ryan – two of the most talented writers I know – for their advice and friendship. Sarah Webb and David Maybury for their constant guidance. Sarwat Chadda and Phil Earle for giving so generously of their time. Everybody who helped with the research for this book: Corina and the team at *Kiss Magazine*, Kieran for his expert opinion and Liz Maybury for her detailed emails. Catherine, Jerry and Kevin for giving me a place to escape to. The Mighty Stef, one of Dublin's best musicians, for allowing me to use his name. All the book buyers, booksellers and librarians who support my books especially Maria, Lisa, Joan and Lisa in Drogheda, Joan, Aisling, Anne and Marianne in Kildare and David O'Callaghan. The book bloggers who mentioned me in the beginning, including Leanna, Precious, Rachel, Jenny, Elizabeth, Iffath and Kai. Amy-Rose for sitting at my table. My amazing readers for the support, love, tweets, comments and emails. The people in Naas who helped with the launch of *Angel Kiss* – Kate, Jason, Jamie, Aoife and everyone at Barker & Jones bookshop, Eileen in Alice's Restaurant, Conor from Jam Music Company and Brian from Rapple Signs. My friends Laura and Liz for assisting me with the planning and invitations. My cousin Adam for doing the photography and my uncle Paul for being there when I really needed him. A special shout out to Martina, Anthea, Moa, Seán and Sandra. John for the high-fives, the typewriter notebooks and for everything else. My mam, Jean, for the proofreading, the late-night chats and for being one of my best friends. My dad, Joe, for the father-and-daughter days, driving me around the Dublin mountains and always knowing what to do. My brother Liam, who is younger than me but infinitely wiser – thank you for being an inspiration and for not letting me give up. My agent, Faith O'Grady, who has never been anything but amazing; I am very grateful to have my own personal superwoman. And finally everyone at Puffin UK, especially Samantha, Mary, Lindsey and Shannon. This is one dream I don't mind not waking up from.

Read on for the first chapter of
Angel Kiss, the first book about
Jacki King . . .

Chapter 1

I watched the funeral pass by from the window of our cluttered caravan. The renovation of our new cottage was not yet complete, so that summer we were living in a little caravan at the top of our lane, overlooking the winding country road. My mum was among the cluster of darkly clad mourners headed to the graveyard. The body in the coffin was that of Jim Cullen. He was a popular man who had lived in a stone cottage about ten minutes' walk from the village of Avarna. Jim had died suddenly of a heart attack aged seventy-two. He was survived by his wife, Lily, and two children. I'd never met him.

We had been living there only two weeks. Mum had met him several times when she'd been house-hunting in Avarna the previous year. It was Jim Cullen who had told her about one particular house that would be coming on the market, as its eccentric owner, a farrier named Alf, was moving to an island off the south coast. The moment she saw it Mum put in an offer and set about selling our house in Dublin. Thanks to the late Jim Cullen she had her idyllic country residence. I'd begged Mum not to accept the job, not to move. I really didn't want to live in the country. I'd screamed and cried and pleaded with her not to make me leave Dublin, but it was no use. She'd never understand just how hard it was for me to leave my friends, my school, my band, everything that was important to me.

When I protested about going to Jim's funeral she presumed it was because I was still mad at her. That was true, but there was another reason. I really disliked funerals. I'd always found myself sensitive to other people's suffering; I seemed to soak up their grief like a sponge. I already felt unwell that day; I had a headache and just knew I wouldn't be able to handle it. I watched until the large crowd passed and then went back to strumming my guitar.

Mum didn't go to the Cullen house for tea afterwards because she only vaguely knew Jim's relatives and didn't want to intrude. I noticed how her eyelids were red when she dozed off later. No doubt she felt just like me: the day's events had reminded her of my dad's funeral. He'd died of a brain tumour when I was nine and even after six years I could still recall the small details of that day. The navy woollen tights that made my legs itch, the smell of the white lilies laid out on the coffin and the grip of my mum's hand on my own small trembling one. He'd been sick for a while, but then suddenly he was gone and the funeral was the first time I began to accept this. Mum and I had learned to cope since then, but we still thought about him all the time. We liked to remember the happy times, how he'd always made us laugh . . . and the way he used to sing along really badly to the radio.

The caravan was a poor replacement for our suburban terraced house, but Mum had assured me that soon we would have a beautifully refurbished cottage, a home unblemished by memories, a fresh start. I missed Dublin so much that I couldn't really appreciate this. I was still coming to terms with the fact that I would have to move to a new school in September, make new friends, find a new band, basically rebuild all these vital parts of my life. I wasn't exactly looking forward to that. I was looking forward to moving into the house though. The caravan was unbelievably cramped, which didn't make things easy between me and Mum when we both needed our own space.

I'd thought living in a caravan would be great fun, kind of like living on a tour bus. And it had been fun . . . for about ten minutes. Mum had rented it online and somehow it looked massive in the images, but in reality it was more like one from an episode of *Father Ted* – except nobody was laughing when it was delivered and we saw how tiny it was. My head almost reached the roof, and I'm only five foot five. At one end there were two single couch beds with some very compact storage space underneath, and there was a table in between them that you could have either up or down. At the other end of the caravan there was a counter top with a hob and a kettle and two cupboards underneath. And in the middle, beside the tiny space that joined the 'bedroom and kitchen' (as the website had put it), was an even tinier bathroom. My bed was the most uncomfortable thing on the planet and I dreaded getting into it.

The night of Jim Cullen's funeral I slept uneasily and awoke from the strangest dream with the scene still vivid in my mind: a drunken man stumbled up a lane, struggling to stay upright. A car pulled up beside him, almost knocking him to the ground. The window rolled down. A hand emerged, clutching a brown leather handbag.

'*Here. Take this and burn it. Do you hear me? Burn it! This and everything in it.*' The hand was trembling but the voice was steady.

'*Why the . . . why the hell should I?*'

'*Because if you don't I'll tell everyone what you did. Do you really want me to tell them about —*'

'*Fine . . . I'll burn the bloody bag. Whose is it anyway?*'

He got no response. The car reversed out, leaving tyre marks in the earth. The drunken man continued up the dark lane, the bag dangling from his right hand.

Once was unsettling enough, but I'd had the same dream nearly every night that week. The way it was so clear in my mind was starting to scare me, and there was one particular thing about it that really freaked me out. I recognized the lane. It was the one that led to our new house. I didn't recognize the men though. I'd never seen them before and I certainly had no desire to. Particularly not the one sitting in the car. His pale eyes held a vicious manic stare that I couldn't forget.

As I tried to get back to sleep, the image of the bag kept coming into my mind. It was a satchel made of chocolate-brown leather, with a little handle as well as a longer strap, and it swung back and forth as the drunken man moved hesitantly along, the moonlight glinting off its gold buckles. The bag looked familiar, like something I'd see when I was searching through vintage shops for clothes.

I hate it when I'm trying to get back to sleep in the middle of the night and my mind won't stop racing. I tried hard to think about something else. Maybe I was so fixated on the dream because I didn't have anything more exciting to distract me. Clearly my anxiety over the move to Avarna had created a recurring nightmare composed of random memories. Once I felt settled I was sure it would go away. *I should spend more time exploring the village*, I thought. *I'm sure there were interesting little corners I hadn't yet discovered. Places like that café and the garden by the river, and that cute little clothes shop. It looked expensive but maybe I'd call in anyway* . . . Eventually, after the distraction of planning my tour of the village, my brain shut down and I fell into a welcome dream-free sleep.

The next morning there was a gorgeous blue sky and I felt a lot better. But we'd run out of milk so I couldn't have cereal. Instead of being annoyed I decided it was fate; I'd wander into the village to get some milk and explore a bit more.

As I walked into the local shop, I heard a loud smack on the window. A fly swatter hit the windowpane with brutal force. I watched as the doomed wasp fell on to the dusty sill, its legs flickering for a moment before it died. The shop owner, Mary Reynolds, stood triumphantly, clasping the blue swatter.

'The little feckers come out earlier every year,' she said as she scooped the tiny corpse into a tissue and dumped it in the bin behind the counter. 'How are you, Jacki? Are you keeping well?'

'Yes, I'm fine, thanks,' I said, trying to be cheerful and heading for the fridge.

Mary knew all of Avarna's residents by name and there was little that happened in the village that she didn't find out about. The first time I'd gone into her shop was only for chewing gum, yet she'd kept me chatting for twenty minutes. She found out my name, my age, that my mum, Rachel, was the new primary school teacher starting in September, that I'd just done my Junior Cert. exams and that I didn't have a boyfriend. In return

I was subjected to her son Nick's entire life story. He was a year older than me, had just finished transition year, was allergic to tomatoes and played electric guitar.

Today I was spared from interrogation as she was soon chatting to another customer. She introduced me to Joe Clancy, owner of the aptly named Clancy's, one of Avarna's four pubs.

'And did you hear Tommy Ford's wife had a baby girl?' said Joe. 'I'm not sure what they called her . . .'

'Chloe Louise, eight pounds twelve ounces, big head of brown hair,' said Mary as she stared at the open window, daring another wasp to fly through it. The shop was uncomfortably warm, as was everywhere in the village during that unusually hot summer.

'Here's hoping she gets her looks from her mother,' said Joe. 'That fella Tommy has a face like a melted welly.'

'You're terrible,' said Mary with a laugh.

I smiled to myself. You couldn't help liking Mary, in spite of her knack for getting information out of everyone who came into the shop.

'Anyway, I better be off,' said Joe. He sauntered out with an ice-cream cone in his hand and a folded newspaper tucked under his elbow.

I checked the selection of biscuits, searching for my favourites.

'Nick!' shouted Mary. There was silence. 'Nick!' she bellowed again. A few moments later her son emerged from the store-room in the back with a copy of *Kerrang!* magazine in his hand and a disgruntled look on his face. Although I'd heard a lot about him from Mary, this was the first time I'd seen him. He was tall and slim and wore faded blue denims and a black T-shirt. His brown hair was quite long and curled across his forehead. As he came towards us, I could see his striking blue eyes and that he had a few freckles on his cheeks. His arms were strong and tanned.

One syllable echoed silently inside my head: Wow. Nick was gorgeous, even with that grumpy look on his face.

'Nick, I have to go to the wholesaler's, so stay behind the counter, will you?' said Mary. She mustn't have realized we hadn't been introduced.

Nick nodded grudgingly and slumped down on the stool behind the till.

'Bye, Jacki,' said Mary, and then she hurried out the door, taking with her any affection I felt for my ex-boyfriend in Dublin. I took out my purse and approached the counter with my milk and biscuits.

'Hi,' he said.

'Hi.'

I tried to think of something intelligent to say, but failed miserably.

'That's two ninety-five,' said Nick.

'Thanks,' I murmured as I handed him three euro with a slightly shaking hand.

'So, you're Jacki?' he asked as his eyes met mine, and he dropped the change into my palm. My insides jolted when I heard him say my name.

'Eh . . . yeah. You must be Nick.' There were a few moments of silence. I tried to think of something to say. Anything at all. But nothing came.

'So how are you finding Avarna so far?'

'Yeah it's . . . it's cool.' Avarna was a lot of things, but cool certainly was not one of them. Why did I have to say cool? Any other word would have done. Any one at all.

'That's good,' said Nick. He smiled at me. I could feel my cheeks warming. The thought that they were undoubtedly bright red made me cringe.

'OK, I better be off,' I said. I wanted to get out of there before I said something else embarrassing.

'See you around,' he said.

And then it came. Whatever possessed me to wave at some-one whose handsome face was a mere metre away from me I will never know. But I did. I gave him a big giant wave. He looked at me a little strangely as I turned away, embarrassed, and rushed out of the shop, my cheeks burning so brightly I could almost feel my new social life going up in flames.

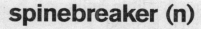

It all started with a Scarecrow.

Puffin is seventy years old.
Sounds ancient, doesn't it? But Puffin has never been
so lively. We're always on the lookout for the next big
idea, which is how it began all those years ago.

Penguin Books was a big idea from the mind of
a man called Allen Lane, who in 1935 invented
the quality paperback and changed the world.
**And from great Penguins, great Puffins grew,
changing the face of children's books forever.**

The first four Puffin Picture Books were hatched in 1940 and the
first Puffin story book featured a man with broomstick arms called
Worzel Gummidge. In 1967 Kaye Webb, Puffin Editor, started the
Puffin Club, promising to **'make children into readers'**.
She kept that promise and over 200,000 children became
devoted Puffineers through their quarterly instalments of
Puffin Post, which is now back for a new generation.

Many years from now, we hope you'll look back and
remember Puffin with a smile. **No matter what your age
or what you're into, there's a Puffin for everyone.**
The possibilities are endless, but one thing is for sure:
whether it's a picture book or a paperback, a sticker book
or a hardback, **if it's got that little Puffin
on it – it's bound to be good.**